Abraham Lincoln

The Presidents Words

SALZWASSER
VERLAG

Abraham Lincoln

The Presidents Words

Reprint of the original, first published in 1865.

1st Edition 2022 | ISBN: 978-3-75259-047-0

Verlag (Publisher): Salzwasser Verlag GmbH, Zeilweg 44, 60439 Frankfurt, Deutschland
Vertretungsberechtigt (Authorized to represent): E. Roepke, Zeilweg 44, 60439 Frankfurt, Deutschland
Druck (Print): Books on Demand GmbH, In de Tarpen 42, 22848 Norderstedt, Deutschland

THE PRESIDENT'S WORDS.

THE

PRESIDENT'S WORDS:

A Selection of Passages

FROM THE

SPEECHES, ADDRESSES, AND LETTERS

OF

ABRAHAM LINCOLN.

"All goes well with us. Every thing seems quiet now."
A. LINCOLN: Telegram, April 2.

BOSTON

1865.

INTRODUCTION.

THE funeral service of the 19th of April, 1865, was the most impressive religious service ever held in this country. By one impulse, the people of the land thronged the churches, which, at the hour of the funeral of the President, were everywhere open. At that hour, more people in this land united in the public worship of God, than ever united in such service on any day before. In Massachusetts, the day has been historical for nearly two centuries. It is now marked by one more association, which will remain in memory till the young children of this generation have grown old and passed away.

This little book, which we call "The President's Words," had its origin in the funeral services of that day. The ministers of different churches, who had to conduct those services, felt, of course, the impossibility of saying any thing which could give any additional precision to the lesson which the hour itself proclaimed. It certainly seemed to me most fit to read from the President's own words, of trust in the people, and faith in God, some of the expressions in which for years he had been the providential teacher of this nation. It was, of course, impossible, on such an occasion, to read more than a few of these.

These selections attracted the attention of the publishers of this volume, who proposed at once to publish a collection of the President's more memorable sayings, and asked me to prepare it for the press. I was very glad to contribute to it such epigrams and aphorisms as I remembered, and had collected, from the addresses by which Mr. Lincoln instructed this country in the principles of its own institutions.

We knew, however, that it was desirable to make as full a collection as possible; and my friend, Mr. John Williams, to whose advice and assistance I am every day indebted, undertook the careful reading of every speech and letter of Mr. Lincoln's, which has been published, with a view to the diligent selection from them all, which he has made and arranged for this volume. To the skill with which he has done this work, the reader is indebted for its close condensation of the most striking thoughts which the President has uttered in his public life.

We have arranged them under five general heads, which will facilitate reference. Within those subdivisions, they are, in general, in the order of time. Every one knows that Mr. Lincoln was taught by experience. "I claim not to have controlled events," he said; "I confess plainly that events have controlled me." It has seemed most fair, therefore, to show, as far as might be, the process of the gradual formation of his opinions. In general, we have printed only brief *memorabilia*, separated even from their immediate connection. The last Inaugural, however, — his last long speech, — and one or two letters, are printed in full.

It has been matter of regret to us, that we could not with propriety put in print the conversational sayings which are so widely accredited to him. But it will be readily admitted, that such a collection, at this time, should not be attempted.

On the day of the funeral, in an address at Concord, Mr. R. W. Emerson thus characterized these brief utterances: —

"He is the author of a multitude of good sayings, so disguised as pleasantries that it is certain they had no reputation at first but as jests; and only later, by the very acceptance and adoption they find in the mouths of millions, turn out to be the wisdom of the hour. I am sure, if this man had ruled in a period of less facility of printing, he would have become mythological in a very few years, like Æsop or Pilpay, or one of the Seven Wise Masters, by his fables and proverbs.

"But the weight and penetration of many passages in his letters, messages, and speeches, hidden now by the very closeness of their application to the moment, are destined hereafter to a wide fame. What pregnant definitions! what unerring common sense! what foresight! and, on great occasions, what lofty, and, more than national, what humane tone! His brief speech at Gettysburg will not easily be surpassed by words on any recorded occasion. This, and one other American speech, that of John Brown to the court that tried him, and a part of Kossuth's speech at Birmingham, can only be compared with each other, and with no fourth."

To such authoritative criticism on the President's words I can add nothing.

EDWARD E. HALE.

BOSTON, May 18, 1865.

POLITICAL SYSTEMS.

THE PRESIDENT'S WORDS.

POLITICAL SYSTEMS.

THE PEOPLE, THE CONSTITUTION, AND THE LAWS.

FREE LABOR.

OUR Government was not established that one man might do with himself as he pleases, and with another man too. . . . I say, that, whereas God Almighty has given every man one mouth to be fed, and one pair of hands adapted to furnish food for that mouth, if any thing can be proved to be the will of Heaven, it is proved by this fact, that that mouth is to be fed by those hands, without being interfered with by any other man, who has also his mouth to feed, and his hands to labor with. I hold, if the Almighty had ever made a set of men that should do all the eating and none of the work, he would have made them with mouths only, and no hands; and if he had ever made another class, that he had intended should do all the work and none of the eating, he would have made them without mouths and with all hands.—*September*, 1859.

HIRED LABOR.

MY understanding of the hired laborer is this: A young man finds himself of an age to be dismissed from parental control; he has for his capital nothing, save two strong hands that God has given him, a heart willing to labor, and a freedom to choose the mode of his work and the manner of his employer; he has got no soil nor shop, and he avails himself of the opportunity of hiring himself to some man who has capital to pay him a fair day's wages for a fair day's work. He is benefited by availing himself of that privilege. He works industriously; he behaves soberly; and the result of a year or two's labor is a surplus of capital. Now he buys land on his own hook; he settles, marries, begets sons and daughters; and, in course of time, he too has enough capital to hire some new beginner. — *September*, 1859.

GOOD TEMPER.

I SHALL endeavor to take the ground I deem most just to the North, the South, the East, the West, and the whole country. I take it, I hope, in good temper, certainly with no malice towards any section. I shall do all that may be in my power to promote a peaceful settlement of all our difficulties. The man does not live who is more devoted to peace than I am. None would do more to preserve it; but it may be necessary to put the foot down firmly. — *February*, 1862.

NATURALIZATION.

AS I understand the spirit of our institutions, it is designed to promote the *elevation* of men. I am therefore hostile to any thing that tends to their debasement. It is well known that I deplore the oppressed condition of the blacks; and it would therefore be very inconsistent for me to look with approval upon any measure that infringes upon the inalienable rights of white men, whether or not they are born in another land, or speak a different language from our own. — *May*, 1859.

SQUATTER SOVEREIGNTY.

I ADMIT that the emigrant to Kansas and Nebraska is competent to govern himself; *but I deny his right to govern any other person, without that person's consent.*

SENATOR OR PRESIDENT.

MR. LINCOLN was urged by some of his friends not to corner Douglas on the point of "unfriendly legislation," because he would surely stand by his doctrine of Squatter Sovereignty, in defiance of the Dred-Scott decision; "and that," said they, "will make him Senator." "That may be," said Mr. Lincoln; "but, if he takes that shoot, he never can be President." — *June*, 1858.

IN INDEPENDENCE HALL.

CAN the country be saved upon the basis of *liberty* and *equality*, as set forth in the Declaration of Independence?

If it can, I will consider myself one of the happiest men in the world, if I can help to save it. If it cannot be saved upon that principle, it will be truly awful. But, if this country cannot be saved without giving up that principle, I was about to say, I would rather be *assassinated* on this spot than surrender it. . . . I have said nothing but what I am willing to live by, and, if it be the pleasure of Almighty God, *die by*. — *February*, 1861.

UTAH.

IT is very plain, the Judge evades the only question the Republicans have ever pressed upon the Democracy in regard to Utah. That question the Judge well knew to be this: "If the people of Utah shall peacefully form a State Constitution, tolerating polygamy, will the Democracy admit them into the Union?"

There is nothing in the United-States Constitution or law against polygamy; and why is it not a part of the Judge's "sacred right of self-government" for the people to have it, or rather to keep it, if they choose? These questions, so far as I know, the Judge never answers. It might involve the Democracy to answer them either way,—and they go unanswered.—*June*, 1857.

THE DECLARATION A WRECK.

LET us hear Judge Douglas's view of that part of the Declaration of Independence, which declares that "all men are created equal." Here it is: "No man can vindicate the character, motives, and conduct of the signers of the Declaration of Independence, except upon the hypothesis that they referred to the white race alone, and not to the African, when they declared all men to have been created equal; that they were speaking of British subjects on this continent, being equal to British subjects born and residing in Great Britain." . . . My good friends, read that carefully over, some leisure hour, and ponder well upon it: see what a mere wreck, mangled ruin, it makes of our once-glorious Declaration of Independence. . . . I had thought the Declaration promised something better than the condition of British subjects; but, no: it only meant that we should be *equal* to them in their own oppressed and *unequal* condition. According to that, it gave no promise, that, having kicked off the king and lords of Great Britain, we should not at once be saddled with a king and lords of our own. . . . I understand, you are preparing to celebrate the "Fourth" to-morrow week. . . . Suppose, after you read the Declaration once, in the old-fashioned way, you read it once more, with Judge Douglas's version. It will run thus: "We hold these truths to be self-evident, that all British subjects who were on this continent eighty-one years ago were created equal to all British subjects born and *then* residing in Great Britain. — *June*, 1857.

PATIENT.

THERE is one other thing I will say to you, in this relation. It is but my opinion: I give it to you without a fee. It is my opinion, that it is for you to take him, or be defeated; and that, if you *do* take him, you *may* be defeated. You will merely be beaten if you do *not* take him. We, the Republicans, and others forming the opposition of the country, intend to "stand by our guns," to be patient and firm, and, in the long-run, to beat you, whether you take him or not. We know, that, before we fairly beat you, we have to beat you both together. We know that you are "all of a feather," and that we have to beat you all together; and we expect to do it. We don't intend to be very impatient about it. We mean to be as deliberate and calm about it as it is possible to be, but as firm and resolved as it is possible for men to be.—*August*, 1858.

HOW DID THE FATHERS ACT?

I SEE, in the Judge's speech here, a short sentence in these words: "Our fathers, when they formed this government under which we live, understood this question just as well, and better, than we do now." That is true; I stick to that. I will stand by Judge Douglas in that to the bitter end.

And now, Judge Douglas, come and stand by me, and truthfully show how they *acted*, understanding it better than we do. All I ask of you, Judge Douglas, is to stick to the proposition, that the men of the Revolution understood this subject better than we do now; ***and, with that better understanding, they acted better than you are trying to act now.*** — *September*, 1859.

BONE OF CONTENTION.

IT is proposed, and carried, to blot out the old dividing line of thirty-four years' standing, and to open the whole of that country to the introduction of slavery. Now this, to my mind, is manifestly unjust. After an angry and dangerous controversy, the parties made friends by dividing the bone of contention. The one party first appropriates her own share, beyond all power to be disturbed in the possession of it, and then seizes the share of the other party. It is as if two starving men had divided their only loaf; the one had hastily swallowed his half, and then grabbed the other's half just as he was putting it to his mouth. — *October*, 1854.

NO MAN IS GOOD ENOUGH TO GOVERN ANOTHER MAN, WITHOUT THAT MAN'S CONSENT.

BUT one argument in the support of the repeal of the Missouri Compromise is still to come. That argument is "the sacred right of self-government." It seems our distinguished Senator has found great difficulty in getting his antagonists, even in the Senate, to meet him fairly on this argument. Some poet has said, "Fools rush in where angels fear to tread."

At the hazard of being thought one of the fools of this quotation, I meet that argument,—I rush in,—I take that bull by the horns. . . . I say that, that no man is good enough to govern another man *without that other's consent.* I say, this is the leading principle, the sheet-anchor of American Republicanism. Our Declaration of Independence says: "That, to secure these rights, governments are instituted among men, DERIVING THEIR JUST POWERS FROM THE CONSENT OF THE GOVERNED." Now, the relation of master and slave is, *pro tanto*, a total violation of their principle. The master not only governs the slave without his consent, but he governs him by a set of rules altogether different from those which he prescribes for himself. Allow ALL the governed an equal voice in the government; and that, and that only, is self-government. . . . If it is a sacred right for the people of Nebraska to take and hold slaves there, it is equally their sacred right to buy them where they can buy them cheapest; and that, undoubtedly, will be on the coast of Africa, provided you will consent not to hang them for going there to buy them. . . . He (the African slave-dealer) honestly buys them at the rate of about a red cotton handkerchief a head. This is very cheap; and it is a great abridgment of the "*sacred right of self-government*," to hang men for engaging in this profitable trade. — *October*, 1854.

MEXICAN WAR.

NOW, sir, for the purpose of obtaining the very best evidence as to whether Texas had actually carried her revolution to the place where the hostilities of the present war commenced, let the President answer the interrogatories I proposed. Let him answer fully, fairly, and candidly. Let him answer with *facts*, not arguments. Let him remember he sits where Washington sat; and, so remembering, let him answer as Washington would answer. As a nation *should* not, and the Almighty *will* not, be evaded, so let him attempt no evasion, no equivocation. . . . But, if he *can* not or will not do this; if, on any pretence or no pretence, he shall refuse or omit it, — then I shall be fully convinced of what I more than suspect already, that he is deeply conscious of being in the wrong; that he feels the blood of this war, like the blood of Abel, is crying to heaven against him; that he ordered General Taylor into the midst of a peaceful Mexican settlement purposely to bring on a war; . . . and, trusting to escape scrutiny by fixing the public gaze upon the exceeding brightness of military glory, — that attractive rainbow that rises in showers of blood; that serpent's eye, that charms to destroy, — he plunged into it, and has swept *on* and *on*, till, disappointed in his calculation of the ease with which Mexico might be subdued, he now finds himself, he knows not where.

MR. POLK'S FEVER-DREAM.

HOW like the half-insane mumbling of a fever-dream is the whole war-part of the late message! — at one time, telling us that Mexico has nothing whatever that we can get but territory; at another, showing us how we can support the war by levying contributions on Mexico. . . . As I have before said, he knows not where he is. He is a bewildered, confounded, and miserably perplexed man. God grant he may be able to show there is not something about his conscience more painful than all his mental perplexity!

JOHN BROWN.

JOHN BROWN'S effort was peculiar. It was an attempt by white men to get up a revolt among slaves, in which the slaves refused to participate. In fact, it was so absurd, that the slaves, with all their ignorance, saw plainly enough it could not succeed. . . . An enthusiast broods over the oppression of a people till he fancies himself commissioned by Heaven to liberate them. He ventures the attempt, which ends in little else than in his own execution. Orsini's attempt on Louis Napoleon, and John Brown's attempt at Harper's Ferry, were, in their philosophy, precisely the same. The eagerness to cast blame on Old England in the one case, and on New England in the other, does not disprove the sameness of the two things. — *February*, 1860.

COOL!

BUT you will not abide the election of a Republican President. In that supposed event, you say, you will destroy the Union; and then, you say, the great crime of having destroyed it will be upon us.

That is cool. A highwayman holds a pistol to my ear, and mutters through his teeth, "Stand and deliver, or I shall kill you; and then you will be a murderer!" To be sure, what the robber demanded of me—my money—was my own, and I had a clear right to keep it: but it was no more my own than my vote is my own; and the threat of death to me, to extort my money, and the threat of destruction to the Union, to extort my vote, can scarcely be distinguished in principle.—*February*, 1860.

WHAT WILL SATISFY THEM?

IT is exceedingly desirable that all parts of this great confederacy shall be at peace, and in harmony one with another. Let us Republicans do our part to have it so. Even though much provoked, let us do nothing through passion and ill-temper. Even though the Southern people will not so much as listen to us, let us calmly consider their demands, and yield to them, if, in our deliberate view of our duty, we possibly can. Judging by all they say and do, and by the subject and nature of their controversy with us, let us determine, if we can, what will satisfy them. — *February*, 1860.

INSURRECTIONS.

YOU charge that we stir up insurrections among your slaves. We deny it; and what is your proof? Harper's Ferry! John Brown! John Brown was no Republican; and you have failed to implicate a single Republican in his Harper's Ferry enterprise. If any member of our party is guilty in that matter, you know it, or you do not know it. If you *do* know it, you are inexcusable to not designate the man, and prove the fact. If you do *not* know it, you are inexcusable to assert it, and especially to persist in the assertion after you have tried and failed to make the proof. You need not be told, that persisting in a charge which one does not know to be true, is simply malicious slander. — *February*, 1860.

THE CRISIS WAS ARTIFICIAL.

WHAT, then, is the matter with them (the South)? Why all this excitement? Why all these complaints? As I said before, this crisis is all artificial. It has no foundation in fact. It was not "argued up," as the saying is, and cannot therefore be argued down. Let it alone, and it will go down of itself. — *February*, 1861.

POLICY OF THE FATHERS.

YOU say we have made the slavery question more prominent than it formerly was. We deny it. We admit that it is more prominent; but we deny that we made it so. It was not we, but you, who discarded the old policy of the fathers. We resisted, and still resist, your innovation; and thence comes the greater prominence of the question. Would you have that question reduced to its former proportions? Go back to that old policy. What has been will be again, under the same conditions. If you would have the peace of the old times, re-adopt the precepts and policy of the old times. — *February*, 1860.

UNION.

PHYSICALLY speaking, we cannot separate. We cannot remove our respective sections from each other, and build an impassable wall between them. A husband and wife may be divorced, and go out of the presence and beyond the reach of each other; but the different parts of our country cannot do this. They cannot but remain face to face; and intercourse, either amicable or hostile, must continue between them. — *March*, 1861.

CONTRACTS.

IF the United States be not a Government proper, but an association of States in the nature of contract merely, can it, as a contract, be peaceably unmade by less than all the parties who made it? One party to a contract may violate it, break it, so to speak; but does it not require all to lawfully rescind it? — *March*, 1861.

TWO HEADS OR ONE.

IT has been said that one bad general is better than two good ones; and the saying is true, if taken to mean no more than that an army is better directed by a single mind, though inferior, than by two superior ones at variance and cross-purposes with each other. — *December*, 1861.

KEEP COOL.

MY countrymen, and all, think calmly and *well* upon this whole subject. Nothing valuable can be lost by taking time. If there be an object to hurry any of you, in hot haste, to a step which you would never take deliberately, that object will be frustrated by taking time; but no good object can be frustrated by it. — *March*, 1861.

NOT FOR US IS AGAINST US.

THE good old maxims of the Bible are applicable, and truly applicable, to human affairs; and in this, as in many other things, we may say here, that "he who is not for us is against us." "He who gathereth not with us, scattereth."

I should be glad to have some of the many good and able and noble men of the South, to place themselves where we can confer upon them the high honor of an election, upon one or other end of our ticket. It would do my soul good to do that thing. It would enable us to teach them, that, inasmuch as we select one of their own number to carry out their principles, we are free from the charge, that we mean more than we say.—*September*, 1859.

THE ISSUE IS WITH THE SOUTH.

IN *your* hands, my dissatisfied fellow-countrymen, and not in *mine*, is the momentous issue of civil war. The Government will not assail *you*. You can have no conflict, without being *yourselves* the aggressors. *You* have no *oath*, registered in heaven, to destroy the Government; while I shall have the most solemn one to "preserve, protect, and defend it."—*March*, 1861.

COERCION AND INVASION.

BUT if the United States should merely hold and retake its own forts and other property, and collect the duties on foreign importations, or even withhold the mails from places where they are habitually violated, would any, or all these things, be "invasion" or "coercion"? Do our professed lovers of the Union, but who spitefully resolve that they will resist coercion and invasion, understand that such things as these on the part of the United States would be coercion or invasion of a State? If so, their ideas of means to preserve the object of their affections would seem exceedingly thin and airy. If sick, the little pills of the homœopathists would be much too large for it to swallow. In their view, the Union, as a family relation, would seem to be no regular marriage, but a sort of "free-love" arrangement, to be maintained only on "passional attraction." — *February*, 1861.

THE RULE OF THE MINORITY IS ANARCHY OR DESPOTISM.

PLAINLY the central idea of secession is the essence of anarchy. A majority, held in restraint by constitutional checks and limitations, and always changing easily with deliberate changes of popular opinions and sentiments, is the only true sovereign of a free people. Whoever rejects it, does, of necessity, fly to *anarchy* or to *despotism*. Unanimity is impossible; the rule of a minority, as a permanent arrangement, is wholly inadmissible; so that, rejecting the majority's principle, *anarchy* and despotism, in some form, is all that is left. — *March* 4, 1861.

THE OBLIGATION.

ALL members of Congress swear their support to the *whole* Constitution,—to *this* provision as well as any other. To this proposition, then, that slaves, whose cases come within the terms of this clause, "shall be delivered up," their oaths are unanimous. Now, if they would make the effort, in good temper, could they not, with nearly equal unanimity, frame and pass a law by means of which to keep *good* that unanimous oath?—*March*, 1861.

HOW SHOULD IT BE KEPT?

THERE is some difference of opinion, whether this clause should be enforced by National or by State authority; but, surely, that difference is not a very material one. If the slave *is* to be surrendered, it can be of but little consequence to him, or to others, by which authority it is done. And should any one, in any case, be content that his oath shall go *unkept*, on a merely unsubstantial controversy as to *how* it shall be kept?—*March*, 1861.

LIBERTY'S SAVING CLAUSE.

AGAIN, in any law upon this subject, ought not all the safeguards of liberty, known in civilized and human jurisprudence, to be introduced, so that a *free* man be not, in any case, surrendered as a *slave?* And might it not be well, at the same time, to provide by law for the enforcement of that clause in the Constitution which guarantees, that "*the citizens of each State shall be entitled to all the privileges and immunities of citizens in the several States.*" —*March*, 1861.

TO THE LAWS AND THE CONSTITUTION.

I TAKE the official oath, to-day, with no mental reservations, and with no purpose to construe the Constitution or laws by any hypercritical rules. And, while I do not choose now to specify particular acts of Congress as proper to be enforced, I do suggest, that it will be much safer for all, both in official and private stations, to conform to and abide by *all* those acts which stand unrepealed, than to violate *any* of them, trusting to find impunity in having them held to be unconstitutional.—*March*, 1861.

ARE THE DECISIONS IN THE SUPREME COURT IRREVOCABLE?

WHILE it is obviously possible that a decision in the Supreme Court may be erroneous in any given case, still the evil effect following it, being limited to that particular case, with the chance that it may be overruled, and never become a precedent for other cases, can better be borne than could the evils of a different practice. At the same time, the candid citizen must confess, that, if the policy of the Government upon vital questions affecting the whole people is to be *irrevocably* fixed by decisions of the SUPREME COURT, the instant they are made in ordinary litigation between parties in personal actions, the people will have ceased to be their own rulers; having, to that extent, practically resigned their government into the hands of that eminent tribunal. — *March*, 1861.

NO COMPROMISE.

I WILL suffer death before I will consent, or advise my friends to consent, to any concession or compromise which looks like buying the privilege of taking possession of the Government, to which we have a constitutional right; because, whatever I might think of the merit of the various propositions before Congress, I should regard any concession, in the face of menace, as the destruction of the Government itself, and a consent, on all hands, that our system shall be brought down to a level with the existing disorganized state of affairs in Mexico. But this thing will hereafter be, as it is now, in the hands of the people; and if they desire to call a convention to remove any grievances complained of, or to give new guarantees for the permanence of vested rights, it is not mine to oppose. — *January*, 1861.

FAITH, HOPE, AND LOVE.

I AM loath to close. We are not *enemies*, but *friends*. We must *not* be enemies. Though passion may have *strained*, it must not *break* our bonds of affection. THE MYSTIC CHORDS OF MEMORY, STRETCHING FROM EVERY BATTLE-FIELD AND PATRIOT GRAVE TO EVERY LIVING HEART AND HEARTH-STONE ALL OVER THIS BROAD LAND, WILL YET SWELL THE CHORUS OF THE UNION, WHEN AGAIN TOUCHED, AS SURELY THEY WILL BE, BY THE BETTER ANGELS OF OUR NATURE. — *March*, 1861.

READ FOR THEMSELVES.

NOT having as yet seen occasion to change, it is now my purpose to pursue the course marked out in the Inaugural Address. I commend a careful consideration of the whole document, as the *best* expression I can give of my purposes. As I then and therein said, I now repeat. — *April*, 1861.

STANTON AND McCLELLAN.

FELLOW-CITIZENS, — I believe there is no precedent for my appearing before you on this occasion; but it is also true, that there is no precedent for your being here yourselves; and I offer, in justification of myself and of you, that, upon examination, I have found nothing in the Constitution against it. . . . General McClellan's attitude is such that, in the very selfishness of his nature, he cannot but wish to be successful, and I hope he will; and the Secretary of War is in precisely the same situation. . . . General McClellan has sometimes asked for things that the Secretary of War did not give him. General McClellan is not to blame for asking what he wanted and needed; and the Secretary of War is not to blame for not giving when he had none to give.—*August*, 1862.

GOD'S REVELATIONS.

THE subject presented in the memorial is one upon which I have thought much for weeks past, and I may even say for months. I am approached with the most opposite opinions and advice, and that by religious men, who are equally certain that they represent the divine will. I am sure that either the one or the other class is mistaken in that belief, and perhaps, in some respect, both. I hope it will not be irreverent for me to say, that if it is probable that God would reveal his will to others, on a point so connected with my duty, it might be supposed he would reveal it directly to me; for, unless I am more deceived in myself than I often am, it is my earnest desire to know the will of Providence in this matter. *And, if I can learn what it is, I will do it.* These are not, however, the days of miracles; and I suppose it will be granted, that I am not to expect a direct revelation. *I must study the plain, physical facts of the case,* ascertain what is possible, and learn what appears to be wise and right.—*Sept.* 13, 1862.

HOW WILL THE BORDER STATES FEEL ABOUT THE PROCLAMATION OF EMANCIPATION?

I WILL mention another thing, though it meet only your scorn and contempt. There are fifty thousand bayonets in the Union army from the Border Slave States. It would be a serious matter, if, in consequence of a proclamation such as you desire, they should go over to the rebels. I do not think they all would, — not so many as a year ago, or as six months ago, — not so many to-day as yesterday. Every day increases their Union feeling. They are also getting their pride enlisted, and want to beat the rebels. Let me say one thing more: I think you should admit that we have already an important principle, to rally and unite the people on, in the fact that Constitutional government is at stake. This is a fundamental idea, going down as deep as any thing. — *September*, 1862.

IFS AND BUTS.

THE man who stands by and says nothing, when the peril of his Government is discussed, cannot be misunderstood. If not hindered, he is sure to help the enemy; much more, if he talks ambiguously, talks for his country with "buts" and "ifs" and "ands." . . . Those now occupying the very highest places in the rebel war service were all within the power of the Government since the rebellion began, and were nearly as well known to be traitors then as now. Unquestionably, if we had seized and held them, the insurgent cause would be much weaker. But no one of them had then committed any crime defined in the law. Every one of them, if arrested, would have been discharged on *habeas corpus*, were the writ allowed to operate. In view of these and similar cases, I think the time not unlikely to come when I shall be blamed for having made too few arrests, rather than too many. —*June*, 1863.

VALLANDIGHAM.

LONG experience has shown, that armies cannot be maintained unless desertions shall be punished by the severe penalty of death. The case requires, and the Law and the Constitution sanction, this punishment. *Must I shoot a simple-minded soldier-boy who deserts, while I must not touch a hair of the wily agitator who induces him to desert?* — *July*, 1862.

MILITARY ELECTIONS.

EXECUTIVE MANSION, WASHINGTON, Nov. 21, 1862.

DEAR SIR, — Dr. Kennedy, bearer of this, has some apprehension that Federal officers, not citizens of Louisiana, may be set up as candidates for Congress in that State. In my view, there could be no possible object in such an election. . . . To send a parcel of Northern men here as representatives, elected, as would be understood (and perhaps really so), at the point of the bayonet, would be disgraceful and outrageous; and, were I a member of Congress here, I would vote against admitting any such man to a seat.

Yours very truly, A. LINCOLN.

HON. G. F. SHEPLEY.

MISSOURI RADICALS.

FROM time to time, I have done and said what appeared to me proper to do and say. The public knows it well. It obliges nobody to follow me; and, I trust, it obliges me to follow nobody. The Radicals and Conservatives each agree with me in some things, and disagree in others. I could wish both to agree with me in all things; for then they would agree with each other, and would be too strong for any foe from any quarter. They, however, choose to do otherwise; and I do not question their right. I, too, shall do what seems to be my duty. . . . It is my duty to hear all; but at last I must, within my sphere, judge what to do and what to forbear. — *October*, 1863.

HABEAS CORPUS.

THE public safety renders it necessary that the grounds of these arrests should at present be withheld; but at the proper time they will be made public. . . . In no case has an arrest been made on mere suspicion, or through personal or partisan animosities; but, in all cases, the Government is in possession of tangible and unmistakable evidence, which will, when made public, be satisfactory to every loyal citizen.

THE FOUR SIDES.

THE dissensions between Union men in Missouri are due solely to a factious spirit which is exceedingly reprehensible. The two parties ought to have their heads knocked together. Either would rather see the defeat of their adversary than that of Jefferson Davis.

We are in civil war. In such cases there always is a main question; but, in this case, that question is a perplexing compound, — Union and slavery. It becomes a question, not of two sides merely, but of at least four sides, even among those who are for the Union, saying nothing of those who are against it. Thus, those who are for the Union *with*, but *not without*, slavery; those for it *without*, but not *with;* those for it *with* or *without*, but prefer it *with;* and those for it *with* or *without*, but prefer it *without*. — *May*, 1863.

FREMONT, BUTLER, AND SIGEL.

IN reply to a delegation, the President said, that it may be a misfortune for the nation that he was elected President. But, having been elected by the people, he meant to be President, and perform his duty according to his best understanding, if he had to die for it. . . . It was a mistake to suppose, that Generals Fremont, Butler, and Sigel were "systematically kept out of command:" on the contrary, he fully appreciated their merits. By their own actions they had placed themselves in the positions they occupied. He was not only willing, but anxious, to place them again in command, as soon as he could find spheres of action for them without doing injustice to others; but that, at present, he "had more pegs than holes to put them in."—1863.

REMOVAL OF GENERAL CURTIS.

YOUR despatch of to-day is just received. It is very painful to me that you, in Missouri, cannot, or will not, settle your factional quarrel among yourselves. I have been tormented with it beyond endurance, for months, by both sides. Neither side pays the least respect to my appeals to your reason. I am now compelled to take hold of the case.—*March*, 1863.

THREE WAYS TO MAKE PEACE.

TO those who are dissatisfied with me, I would say, You desired peace, and you blame me that we do not have it. But how can we attain it? There are but three conceivable ways: First, to suppress the rebellion by force of arms. This I am trying to do. Are you for it? If you are, so far we are agreed. If you are not for it, a second way is to give up the Union. I am against this. Are you for it? If you are, you should say so plainly. If you are not for force, nor yet for dissolution, there only remains some imaginable compromise.—*August*, 1863.

TO GENERAL SCHOFIELD.

LET your military measures be strong enough to repel the invaders and keep the peace, and not so strong as to unnecessarily harass and persecute the people. It is a difficult *rôlé;* and so much greater will be the honor, if you perform it well. If both factions, or neither, shall abuse you, you will probably be about right. Beware of being assailed by one, and praised by the other.—*May*, 1863.

Allow no part of the military under your command to be engaged in either returning fugitive slaves, or in forcing or enticing slaves from their homes; and, so far as is practicable, enforce the same forbearance upon the people.

Allow no one to enlist colored troops, except upon orders from you, or from here through you.

Allow no one to assume the functions of confiscating property, under the law of Congress, or otherwise, except upon orders from here.

At elections, see that those, and only those, are allowed to vote, who are entitled to do so by the laws of Missouri. — *October*, 1863.

DR. McPHEETERS.

I HAVE never interfered, nor thought of interfering, as to who shall or shall not preach in any church; nor have I knowingly or believingly tolerated any one else to interfere by my authority. . . . If, after all, what is now sought is to have me put Dr. Mc. back over the heads of a majority of his own congregation, that too will be declined. I will not have control of any church or any side. — *December*, 1863.

COMPROMISE.

I DO not believe that any compromise, embracing the maintenance of the Union, is now possible. All that I learn tends to a directly opposite belief. The strength of the rebellion is its military, — its army. In any compromise, we should waste time, which the enemy would improve to our disadvantage; and that would be all. — *August*, 1863.

FOURTH OF JULY, 1863.

FELLOW-CITIZENS, — I am very glad indeed to see you to-night, and yet I will not say I thank you for this call; but I do most sincerely thank Almighty God for the occasion on which you have called. How long ago is it? Eighty-odd years since, on the Fourth of July, for the first time in the history of the world, a nation by its representatives assembled, and declared as a self-evident truth "that all men are created equal." That was the birthday of the United States of America. Since then, the Fourth of July has had several very peculiar recognitions. The two men most distinguished in the framing and support of the Declaration were Thomas Jefferson and John Adams, — the one having penned it, and the other sustained it most forcibly in debate, — the only two of the fifty-five who signed it, and were elected Presidents of the United States. Precisely fifty years after they put their hands to the paper, it pleased Almighty God to take both from this stage of action. This was indeed an extraordinary and remarkable event in our history.

Another President, five years later, was called from this stage of existence, on the same day and month of the year; and now, on this last Fourth of July, just passed, when we have a gigantic rebellion, at the bottom of which is an effort to overthrow the principle that all men were created equal, we have the surrender of a most powerful position and army on that very day. And not only so, but in a succession of battles in Pennsylvania, near to us, through three days, so rapidly fought that they might be called one great battle, on the first, second, and third of the month of July; and, on the fourth, the cohorts of those who opposed the Declaration that "all men are created equal," turned tail and ran. — *July*, 1863.

THE WAR POWER THE ONLY RECONSTRUCTIONIST.

IN the midst of other cases, however important, we must not lose sight of the fact, that the *war power* is still our main reliance. To that power alone we can look, yet for a time, to give confidence to the people, in the contested regions, that the insurgent power will not again overrun them. Until that confidence shall be established, little can be done anywhere for what is called *reconstruction*.

Hence our chiefest care must still be directed to the army and navy, who have, thus far, borne their harder part so nobly and well. And it may be esteemed fortunate, that, in giving the greatest efficiency to these indispensable arms, we do also honorably recognize the gallant men, from commander to sentinel, who compose them, and to whom, more than to others, the world must stand indebted for the home of freedom, disinthralled, regenerated, enlarged, and perpetuated. — *December*, 1863.

RIGHT.

WHEN the time comes, I shall take the ground that I think is right, — right for the North, for the South, for the East, for the West, — for the whole country. And, in doing so, I hope to feel no necessity pressing upon me to say any thing in conflict with the Constitution; in conflict with the Union of these States; in conflict with the perpetuation of the liberties of this people, — or any thing in conflict with any thing whatever that I have ever given you reason to expect from me. And now, my friends, have I said enough? (Cries of "No, no," and "Three cheers for Lincoln.") Now, my friends, there appears to be a difference of opinion between you and me; and I really feel called upon to decide the question myself. — *February*, 1863.

THE DRAFT.

WE are contending with an enemy, who, as I understand, drives every able-bodied man he can reach into his ranks, very much as a butcher drives bullocks into a slaughter-pen. No time is wasted, no argument is used. . . . I do not object to abide a decision of the United-States Supreme Court, or of the judges thereof, on the constitutionality of the draft-law. In fact, I should be willing to facilitate the obtaining of it. But I cannot consent to lose the time while it is being obtained. — *August*, 1863.

RE-NOMINATION.

Don't Swap Horses while Crossing the River.

I AM not insensible at all to the personal compliment there is in this; and yet I do not allow myself to believe, that any but a small portion of it is to be appropriated as a personal compliment. . . . The part I am entitled to appropriate as a compliment is only that part which I may lay hold of as being the opinion of the Convention and the League, that I am not entirely unworthy to be intrusted with the place which I have occupied for the last three years. But I do not allow myself to suppose, that either the Convention or the League have concluded to decide that I am either the greatest or best man in America; but rather they have concluded, *that it is not best to swap horses while crossing the river;* and have further concluded, *that I am not so poor a horse, that they might not make a botch of it in trying to swap.* — *June*, 1864.

TO WHOM IT MAY CONCERN.

ANY proposition which embraces the restoration of peace, the integrity of the whole Union, and the abandonment of Slavery, and which comes by and with an authority that can control the armies now at war against the United States, will be received and considered by the Executive Government of the United States, and will be met by liberal terms on other substantial and collateral points; and the bearer or bearers thereof shall have safe conduct both ways. — *July*, 1864.

SUCCESS OF GRANT BETTER THAN BALTIMORE CONVENTIONS.

THE hardest of all speeches I have to answer is a serenade. I never know what to say on such occasions. I suppose you have done me this kindness in connection with the action of the Baltimore Convention, which has recently taken place, and with which, of course, I am very well satisfied. What we want, still more than Baltimore Conventions or Presidential elections, is success under General Grant. I propose that you constantly bear in mind, that the support you owe to the brave officers and soldiers in the field is of the very first importance; and we should, therefore, bend all our energies to that point. Now, without detaining you any longer, I propose that you help me to close up what I am now saying with three rousing cheers for General Grant and the officers and soldiers under his command. — *June*, 1864.

WHICH LINE HE FIGHTS ON.

IT is a pertinent question, often asked in the mind privately, and from one to the other, When is the war to end? Surely I feel as deep an interest in this question as any other can; but I do not wish to name a day, a month, or a year, when it is to end. . . . We accepted this war for an object, — a worthy object; and the war will end when that object is attained. Under God, I hope it never will end until that time. Speaking of the present campaign, General Grant is reported to have said, "I am going through on this line, if it takes all summer." This war has taken three years; it was begun, or accepted, upon the line of restoring the national authority over the whole national domain; and for the American people, as far as my knowledge enables me to speak, I say, we are going through on *this line*, if it takes three years more. — *June*, 1864.

THE CONSTITUTION.

WAS it possible to lose the nation, and yet preserve the Constitution? By general law, life *and* limb must be protected; yet often a *limb* must be amputated to save a *life*: but a *life* is never wisely given to save a *limb*. I felt that measures, otherwise unconstitutional, might become lawful by becoming indispensable to the preservation of the nation. Right or wrong, I assumed this ground, and now avow it. I could not feel, that, to the best of my ability, I had ever tried to preserve the Constitution, if, to save slavery, or any minor matter, I should permit the wreck of Government, Country, and Constitution, altogether. — *April*, 1864.

TAKE YOUR TIME.

GENTLEMEN, — The general aspect of your movement I cordially approve. In regard to particulars, I must ask time to deliberate, as the work of amending the Constitution should not be done hastily. I will carefully examine your paper, in order more fully to comprehend its contents than is possible from merely hearing it read, and will take such action upon it as my responsibility to our Maker and our country demands. — *January*, 1864.

STRENGTH OF REPUBLICS.

IS there in all republics this inherent and fatal weakness? Must a Government of necessity be too strong for the liberties of its own people, or too weak to maintain its own existence? — *July*, 1861.

OFFICIAL OATH.

ARE all the laws but one to go unexecuted, and the Government itself go to pieces, but that one be violated? Even in such a case, would not the official oath be broken, if the Government should be overthrown, when it was believed that disregarding that single law would tend to preserve it? — *July*, 1861.

SLAVERY AND ANTISLAVERY.

SLAVERY AND ANTISLAVERY.

KANSAS AND NEBRASKA.—DRED-SCOTT DECISION. THE REBELLION.

THE NEGRO.

THERE will be some black men who can remember, that, with silent tongue and clenched teeth and steady eye and well-poised bayonet, they have helped mankind on to this great consummation; while, I fear, there will be some white ones unable to forget, that, with malignant heart and deceitful speech, they have striven to hinder it.—*August*, 1863.

NEBRASKA BILL.

THE Nebraska bill finds no model in any law, from Adam till to-day. As Phillips says of Napoleon, the Nebraska act is grand, gloomy, and peculiar; wrapped in the solitude of its own originality, without a model, and without a shadow upon the earth.—*October*, 1854.

SLAVERY.

THE shepherd drives the wolf from the sheep's throat, for which the sheep thanks the shepherd as a *liberator;* while the wolf denounces him, for the same act, as the destroyer of liberty, especially as the sheep was a black one. Plainly, the sheep and the wolf are not agreed upon the word "liberty;" and precisely the same difference prevails to-day among us human creatures, even in the North, and all professing to love liberty. — *April,* 1864.

WHAT IS AND WHAT MAY BE.

AS this subject is no other than part and parcel of the larger question of domestic slavery, I wish to *make* and to *keep* the distinction between the *existing* institution, and the *extension* of it, so broad and so clear that no honest man can misunderstand me, and no dishonest one successfully misrepresent me. . . . I have no prejudice against the Southern people. They are just what we would be in their situation. If slavery did not now exist among them, they would not introduce it. If it did now exist among us, we should not instantly give it up. This I believe of the masses, North and South. Doubtless there are individuals, on both sides, who would not hold slaves under any circumstances; and others who would gladly introduce slavery anew, if it were out of existence. We know that some Southern men do free their slaves, go North, and become tip-top abolitionists; while some Northern men go South, and become most cruel slave-masters. — *October*, 1854.

POPULAR SOVEREIGNTY.

IF any man can show how the people of Kansas have a better right to slaves because they want them, than the people of Georgia have to buy them in Africa, I want him to do it. I think it cannot be done. If it is "Popular Sovereignty" for the people to have slaves because they want them, it is "Popular Sovereignty" for them to buy them in Africa because they desire to do so. — *September*, 1859.

FREE-STATE DEMOCRAT.

ALLOW me to barely whisper my suspicion, that there were no such things in Kansas as "Free-State Democrats;" that they were altogether mythical, good only to figure in newspapers and speeches in the Free States. If there should prove to be one real, living Free-State Democrat in Kansas, I suggest that it might be well to catch him, and stuff and preserve his skin, as an interesting specimen of that soon-to-be-extinct variety of the genus Democrat. — *June*, 1857.

HUNTER'S PROCLAMATION.

WHETHER it be competent for me, as Commander-in-Chief of the army and navy, to declare the slaves of any State or States free; and whether, at any time or in any case, it shall have become a necessity indispensable to the maintenance of the government to exercise such supposed power, — are questions which, under my responsibility, I reserve to myself, and which I cannot feel justified in leaving to the decision of commanders in the field. — *June*, 1862.

EQUAL RIGHTS.

I AGREE with Judge Douglas, the negro is not my equal in many respects, certainly not in color, perhaps not in moral or intellectual endowments. But in the right to eat the bread, without leave of anybody else, which his own hand earns, *he is my equal, and the equal of Judge Douglas, and the equal of every living man.* Any thing that argues me into his idea of perfect social and political equality with the negro, is but a specious and fantastic arrangement of words, by which a man can prove a *horse-chestnut* to be a *chestnut-horse.* — *September*, 1859.

SACRED RIGHT OF SLAVERY.

THE plain, unmistakable spirit of the fathers of the Republic towards slavery was hostility to the PRINCIPLE, and toleration ONLY BY NECESSITY.

But *now* it is to be transformed into a "SACRED RIGHT." Nebraska brings it forth, places it on the high road to extension and perpetuity; and, with a pat on its back, says to it, "Go, and God speed you." Henceforth it is to be the chief jewel of the nation, — the very figure-head of the ship of State. Little by little, but steadily as man's march to the grave, we have been giving up the OLD for the NEW faith. Near eighty years ago we began by declaring that "all men are created equal;" but now, from that beginning, we have run down to the other declaration, that for SOME men to enslave OTHERS is a "sacred right of self-government." These principles cannot stand together. They are as opposite as GOD and MAMMON; and whoever holds to the *one*, must despise the *other*.—*October*, 1854.

THE TREE OF GOOD AND EVIL.

IN the course of my main argument, Judge Douglas interrupted me to say, that the principle of the Nebraska bill was very old; that it originated when God made man, and placed good and evil before him, allowing him to choose for himself, being responsible for the choice he should make. At the time, I thought this was merely playful; and I answered it accordingly. But, in his reply to me, he renewed it as a serious argument. In seriousness, then, the facts of this proposition are not true, as stated. God did not place good and evil before man, telling him to make his choice. On the contrary, he *did* tell him there was *one* tree of the fruit of which he should not eat, upon pain of certain death. I should scarcely wish so strong a prohibition against slavery in Nebraska.

But this argument strikes me as not a little remarkable in another particular,—in its strong resemblance to the old argument for the "divine right of kings." By the latter, the king is to do just as he pleases with his white subjects, being responsible to God alone; by the former, the white man is to do just as he pleases with his black slaves, being responsible to God alone. The two things are precisely alike; and it is but natural that they should find similar arguments to sustain them. — *October*, 1854.

SLAVE-DEALER.

YOU have among you a sneaking individual of the class of native tyrants known as the SLAVE-DEALER. He watches your necessities, and crawls up to buy your slave at a speculating price. If you cannot help it, you sell to him; but, if you can help it, you drive him from your door. You despise him utterly. You do not recognize him as a friend, or even as an honest man. Your children must not play with his; they may rollic freely with the little negroes, but not with the "*slave-dealer's*" children. If you are obliged to deal with him, you try to get through the job without so much as touching him. It is common with you to join hands with the men you meet; but with the "*slave-dealer*" you avoid the ceremony,—instinctively shrink from the snaky contact. If he grows rich, and retires from business, you still remember him, and still keep up the bar of non-intercourse upon him and his family. Now, why is this? You do not so treat the man who deals in corn, cattle, or tobacco.—*October*, 1854.

HOGS AND NEGROES.

EQUAL justice to the South, it is said, requires us to consent to the extension of slavery to new countries. That is to say, inasmuch as you do not object to my taking my hog to Nebraska, therefore I must not object to your taking your slave. Now, I admit this is perfectly logical, if there is no difference between hogs and negroes. But, while you thus require me to deny the humanity of the negro, I wish to ask whether you of the South, yourselves, have ever been willing to do as much? ... In 1820 you joined the North, almost unanimously, in declaring the African slave-trade *piracy*, and in annexing to it the punishment of death. Why did you do this? If you did not feel that it was wrong, why did you join in providing that men should be hung for it? The practice was no more than bringing wild *negroes* from Africa to sell to such as would buy them. But you never thought of hanging men for catching and selling wild *horses*, wild *buffaloes*, or wild *bears*. — *October*, 1854.

SELFISHNESS AND SLAVERY.

ARGUE as you will, and as long as you will, this is the naked FRONT and ASPECT of the measure; and in this aspect it could not but produce agitation. Slavery is founded in the selfishness of man's nature; opposition to it, in his love of justice. These principles are an eternal antagonism; and when brought into collision, so fiercely as slavery extension brings them, shocks, throes, and convulsions must ceaselessly follow. Repeal the Missouri Compromise; repeal all compromise; repeal the Declaration of Independence; repeal all past history, — you still cannot repeal human nature. It still will be the abundance of man's heart, that slavery extension is wrong; and, out of the abundance of his heart, his mouth will continue to speak. — *October*, 1854.

LIBERTY OF ALL MEN.

FELLOW-COUNTRYMEN, Americans, South as well as North, shall we make no effort to arrest this [the extension of slavery]? Already the liberal party throughout the world express the apprehension, "that the one retrograde institution in America is undermining the principles of progress, and fatally violating the noblest political system the world ever saw." This is not the taunt of enemies, but the warning of friends. Is it quite safe to disregard it,—to despise it? Is there no danger to liberty itself in discarding the earliest practice and first precept of our ancient faith? In our greedy chase to make profit of the negro, let us beware lest "we cancel and tear to pieces" even the white man's charter of freedom.—*October*, 1854.

BOWIE-KNIVES AND BALLOT-BOXES.

SOME Yankees in the East are sending emigrants to Nebraska, to exclude slavery from it; and, so far as I can judge, they expect the question to be decided by *voting* in some way or other. But the Missourians are awake too. They are within a stone's throw of the contested ground. They hold meetings and pass resolutions, in which not the slightest allusion to *voting* is made. They resolve that slavery already exists in the territory; that more shall go there; that they, remaining in Missouri, will protect it; and that Abolitionists shall be hung or driven away. Through all this, *bowie-knives* and *six-shooters* are seen plainly enough; but never a glimpse of the *ballot-box*.— *October*, 1854.

MISSOURI COMPROMISE.

SOME men, mostly Whigs, who condemn the repeal of the Missouri Compromise, nevertheless hesitate to go for its restoration, lest they be thrown in company with the Abolitionists. Will they allow me as an old Whig to tell them, good-humoredly, that I think this is very silly? Stand with anybody that stands RIGHT. Stand with him while he is right, and PART with him when he goes WRONG. Stand WITH the Abolitionists in restoring the Missouri Compromise, and stand AGAINST him when he attempts to repeal the fugitive-slave law. In the latter case, you stand with the Southern disunionist. What of that? You are still RIGHT. In both cases you are RIGHT. In both cases you oppose the dangerous extremes. In both you stand on middle ground, and hold the ship level and steady. In both you are national, and nothing less than national. This is the good old WHIG ground. To desert such ground because of ANY company is to be less than a WHIG, — less than a MAN, — less than an AMERICAN. — *October*, 1854.

DECLARATION OF INDEPENDENCE.

WHEN Mr. Pettit, in connection with his support of the Nebraska bill, called the Declaration of Independence "a self-evident lie," he only did what consistency and candor require all other Nebraska men to do. Of the forty-odd Nebraska senators who sat present and heard him, no one rebuked him. . . . If this had been said among Marion's men, Southerners though they were, what would have become of the man who said it? If this had been said to the men who captured André, the man who said it would probably have been hung sooner than André was. If it had been said in old Independence Hall, seventy-eight years ago, the very doorkeeper would have throttled the man, and thrust him into the street. — *October*, 1854.

RIGHT AND NECESSITY.

OUR republican robe is soiled,—trailed in the dust. Let us re-purify it. Let us turn and wash it white, in the spirit, if not the blood, of the Revolution. Let us turn slavery from its claims of "moral right" back upon its existing legal rights and its arguments of "necessity." Let us return it to the position our fathers gave it, and there let it rest in peace. Let us re-adopt the Declaration of Independence, and with it the practices and policy which harmonize with it. Let North and South,—let all Americans,—let all lovers of liberty everywhere,—join in the great and good work. If we do this, we shall not only have saved the Union, but we shall have *so* saved it as to make and to keep it for ever *worthy* of the saving. We shall have so saved it that the succeeding millions of free, happy people, the world over, shall rise up, and call us blessed to the latest generations.—*October*, 1854.

POOR WHITES.

WHETHER slavery shall go into Nebraska or other new Territories, is not a matter of exclusive concern to the people who may go there.

The whole nation is interested that the best use shall be made of these Territories. We want them for homes of free white people. This they cannot be, if slavery shall be planted within them. Slave States are places for poor white people to move FROM, not to remove TO. New Free States are the places for poor people to go to, and better their condition. For this use the nation needs these Territories.

. . . There are constitutional relations between the Slave and the Free States which are degrading to the latter. We are under legal obligations to catch and return their runaway slaves to them, — a sort of dirty, disagreeable job, which, I believe, as a general rule, the slaveholders will not perform for one another. — *October*, 1854.

THREE-FIFTHS VOTE.

AFTER showing that each white man in South Carolina is more than the double of any man in Maine, — "Yet," he says . . . "I do not mention this to complain of it. . . It is in the Constitution. . . I stand to it fairly, fully, and firmly. But, when I am told I must leave it altogether to *other people* to say whether new partners are to be bred up and brought into the firm on the same degrading terms against me, I respectfully demur. I insist that, whether I shall be a whole man or only the half of one, in comparison with others, is a question in which I am somewhat concerned, and one which no other man can have a 'sacred right' of deciding for me. If I am wrong in this, — if it really be a 'sacred right of self-government' in the man who shall go to Nebraska to decide whether he will be the EQUAL of me or the DOUBLE of me, then, after he shall have exercised that right, and thereby shall have reduced me to a still smaller fraction of a man than I already am, I should like for some gentleman, deeply skilled in 'sacred rights,' to provide himself with a microscope, and peep about and find out, if he can, what has become of *my* 'sacred rights'! They will surely be too small for detection with the naked eye." — *October*, 1854.

NEW LIGHTS.

THUS, with the author of the Declaration of Independence, did the policy of prohibiting slavery in the Territories originate. . . . But *now* new light breaks upon us. *Now* Congress declares this ought never to have been, and the like of it must never be again. "The sacred right of self-government" is grossly violated by it. We even find some men, who drew their first breath and every other breath of their lives under this very restriction, now live in dread of absolute suffocation, if they should be restricted in the "sacred right" of taking slaves to Nebraska. That *perfect* liberty they sigh for — the liberty of making slaves of other people — Jefferson never thought of, — they never thought of themselves a year ago. How fortunate for them they did not sooner become sensible of their great misery! — *October*, 1854.

SLAVERY IN THE TERRITORIES.

FINALLY, I insist, that, if there is ANY THING which it is the duty of the WHOLE PEOPLE to never intrust to any hands but their own, that thing is the preservation and perpetuity of their own liberties and institutions. And, if they shall think, as I do, that the *extension of slavery* endangers them more than any or all other causes, how recreant to themselves if they submit the question, and with it the fate of their country, to a mere handful of men, bent only on temporary self-interest! If this question of *slavery extension* were an insignificant one, — one having no power to do harm, — it might be shuffled aside in this way; but being, as it is, the great Behemoth of danger, shall the strong grip of the nation be loosened upon him, to intrust him to the hands of such feeble keepers?

I have done with this mighty argument of "self-government."

Go, SACRED THING! *Go in peace.* — *October*, 1854.

EXTENSION OF SLAVERY.

BUT Nebraska is urged as a great Union-saving measure. Well, I too go for saving the Union. Much as I hate slavery, I would consent to the extension of it, rather than see the Union dissolved; just as I would consent to any *great* evil to avoid a *greater* one. But, when I go to Union-saving, I must believe, at least, that the means I employ have some adaptation to the end. To my mind, Nebraska has no such adaptation.

"It hath no relish of salvation in it." It is an aggravation, rather, of the only one thing which ever endangers the Union. . . . It could not but be expected of its author, that it would be looked upon as a measure for the *extension of slavery*, aggravated by a gross breach of faith.

I object to it because the fathers of the republic eschewed and rejected it. . . . They found the institution existing among us, which they could not help, and they cast blame on the British king for having permitted its introduction. BEFORE the Constitution, they prohibited its introduction into the North-western Territory, the only country we owned then free from it. At the framing and adoption of the Constitution, they forbore to so much as mention the word "slave," or "slavery," in the whole instrument. In the provision for the recovery of fugitives, the slave is spoken of as a "PERSON HELD TO SERVICE OR LABOR." . . . Thus the thing is hid away in the Constitution, just as an afflicted man hides away a wen or cancer, which he dares not cut out at once lest he bleed to death; with the promise, nevertheless, that the cutting may begin at the end of a certain time. LESS than this our fathers COULD not do; and MORE they WOULD not do. . . . They hedged and hemmed it in to the narrowest limits of necessity. — *October*, 1854.

GRADUAL EMANCIPATION.

IF all earthly power were given me, I should not know what to do as to the existing institution. My first impulse would be to free all the slaves, and send them to Liberia, — to their own native land. . . . But, if they were all landed there in a day, they would all perish in the next ten days; and there are not surplus shipping and surplus money enough to carry them there in many times ten days. What then? Free them all, and keep them among us as underlings? Is it quite certain that this betters their condition? I think I would not hold one in slavery at any rate; yet the point is not clear enough for me to denounce people upon. What next? Free them, and make them politically and socially our equals? My own feelings will not admit of this; and, if mine would, we well know that those of the great mass of white people will not. A universal feeling, whether well or ill founded, cannot be safely disregarded. We cannot then make them equals. It does seem to me that systems of gradual emancipation might be adopted; but, for their tardiness in this, I will not undertake to judge our brethren of the South. —*October*, 1854.

THE COMPROMISES OF 1850.

IN answer to Douglas's assumption, that they had no connection with one another, and that Illinois came in as a Slave State, &c.: If we do not know these things, we do not know that we ever had a Revolutionary War, or such a chief as Washington. To deny these things is to deny our national axioms, or dogmas at least; and puts an end to all argument. If a man will stand up and assert, and repeat and re-assert, that two and two do *not* make four, I know nothing in the power of argument that can stop him. I think I can answer the Judge, so long as he sticks to the premises; but, when he flies from them, I cannot work an argument into the consistency of a maternal gag, and actually close his mouth with it. In such a case, I can only commend him to the seventy thousand answers just in from Pennsylvania, Ohio, and Indiana. — *October*, 1854.

RUSHING TO ARMS.

OUR Senator objects, that those who oppose him in this measure do not entirely agree with one another. He reminds me, that, in my firm adherence to the constitutional rights of the Slave States, I differ widely from others who are co-operating with me in opposing the Nebraska bill. . . . He should remember, that he took us by surprise — astounded us — by this measure. We were thunder-struck and stunned; and we reeled and fell in utter confusion. But we rose; each fighting; grasping whatever he could first reach, — a scythe, — a pitchfork, — a chopping-axe, — or a butcher's cleaver. We struck in the direction of the sound; and we are rapidly closing in upon him. He must not think to divert us from our purpose, by showing us that our drill, our dress, and our weapons, are not entirely perfect and uniform. When the storm shall be past, he shall find us still AMERICANS; no less devoted to the continued union and prosperity of the country than heretofore. — *October*, 1854.

NEGRO A MAN.

THE Republicans inculcate, with whatever of ability they can, that the negro is a man; that his bondage is cruelly wrong, and that the field of his oppression might not be enlarged. The Democrats deny his manhood; deny, or dwarf to insignificance, the wrong of his bondage; so far as possible, crush all sympathy for him, and cultivate and excite hatred and disgust against him; compliment themselves as Union-savers for doing so, and call the indefinite outspreading of his bondage "a sacred right of self-government." The plainest print cannot be read through a gold eagle; and it will be ever hard to find many men who will send a slave to Liberia and pay his passage, while they can send him to a new country, — Kansas, for instance, — and sell him for fifteen hundred dollars, and the rise. — *June*, 1857.

SLAVEHOLDERS AND AMALGAMATION.

THE very Dred-Scott case affords a strong test as to which party most favors amalgamation, the Republicans or the dear Union-saving Democracy. Dred Scott, his wife, and two daughters, were all involved in the suit. We desired the Court to have held that they were citizens, so far at least as to entitle them to a hearing as to whether they were free or not; and then, also, that they were, in fact and in law, really free. Could we have had our way, the chances of these black girls ever mixing their blood with that of white people, would have been diminished, at least to the extent that it could not have been without their consent. But Judge Douglas is delighted to have them decided to be slaves, and not human enough to have a hearing, even if they were free, and thus left subject to the forced concubinage of their masters, and liable to become the mothers of mulattoes, in spite of themselves; the very state of case that produces nine-tenths of all the mulattoes, all the mixing of blood, in the nation.—*June*, 1857.

THE STONE OF STUMBLING.

THE assertion that "all men are created equal" was of no practical use in effecting our separation from Great Britain; and it was placed in the Declaration, not for that, but for future use. Its authors mean it to be—as, thank God! it is now proving itself—a stumbling-block to all those who, in after-times, might seek to turn a free people back into the hateful paths of despotism. They knew the proneness of prosperity to breed tyrants; and they meant, when such should re-appear in this fair land and commence their vocation, they should find left for them one hard nut to crack.—*June*, 1857.

EQUAL IN RIGHTS.

HE (Douglas) finds the Republicans insisting that the Declaration of Independence includes ALL men, black as well as white, and forthwith boldly denies that it includes negroes at all, and proceeds to argue gravely, that all who contend it does do so only because they want to vote and eat and sleep and marry with negroes! . . . Now, I protest against the counterfeit logic which concludes that, because I do not want a black woman for a slave, I must necessarily want her for a wife. I need not have her for either. I can just leave her alone. In some respects she certainly is not my equal; but in her natural right to eat the bread she earns with her own hands, without asking leave of any one else, she is my equal, and the equal of all others. — *June*, 1857.

DRED-SCOTT DECISION.

WHAT is the Dred-Scott decision? Judge Douglas labors to show that it is one thing, while I think it is altogether different. It is a long opinion; but it is all embodied in this short statement: "The Constitution of the United States forbids Congress to deprive a man of his property without due process of law. The right of property in slaves is distinctly and expressly affirmed in that Constitution: therefore, if Congress shall undertake to say that a man's slave is no longer his slave when he crosses a certain line into a Territory, that is depriving him of his property, without due process of law. — *September*, 1859.

CHIEF-JUSTICE TANEY.

CHIEF-JUSTICE TANEY, after quoting from the Declaration of Independence, says, "The general words above quoted would seem to include the whole human family; and, if they were used in a similar instrument at this day, would be so understood."

The Chief-Justice does not directly assert, but plainly assumes as a fact, that the public estimate of the black man is more favorable now than in the days of the Revolution. This assumption is a mistake. . . . In those days, our Declaration of Independence was held sacred by all, and thought to include all; but now, to aid in making the bondage of the negro universal and eternal, it is assailed, sneered at, and construed, and hawked at and torn, till, if its framers could rise from their graves, they could not at all recognize it. —*June*, 1857.

HOW SHALL WE TREAT THE SOUTH?

WHEN we do, as we say, beat you, you perhaps want to know what we mean to do with you.

We mean to treat you, as near as we possibly can, as Washington, Jefferson, and Madison treated you. We mean to leave you alone, and in no way interfere with your institution. . . . We mean to remember that you are as good as we; that you have as good hearts in your bosoms as other people, or as we claim to have, and treat you accordingly. We mean to marry your girls when we have a chance, — the white ones I mean; and I have the honor to inform you that I once did have a chance in that way. — *September*, 1859.

BLACK AND WHITE.

I HAVE never seen, to my knowledge, a man, woman, or child, who was in favor of producing perfect equality, social and political, between negroes and white men. I recollect of but one distinguished instance that I ever heard of so frequently as to be satisfied of its correctness; and that is the case of Judge Douglas's old friend, Colonel Richard M. Johnson. . . . I have never had the least apprehension that I or my friends would marry negroes, if there was no law to keep them from it; but as Judge Douglas and his friends seem to be in great apprehension that they might, if there were no law to keep them from it, I give him the most solemn pledge, that I will, to the very last, stand by the law of the State which forbids the marrying of white people with negroes. — *September*, 1859.

LOCKED AND BOLTED IN.

ALL the powers of earth seem rapidly combining against him (the negro). Mammon is after him; ambition follows, philosophy follows; and the theology of the day is fast joining the cry. They have him in his prison-house; they have searched his person, and left no prying-instrument with him. One after another they have closed the heavy iron doors upon him; and now they have him, as it were, bolted in with a lock of a hundred keys, which can never be unlocked without the concurrence of every key; the keys in the hands of a hundred different men, and they scattered to a hundred different and distant places; and they stand musing as to what invention, in all the dominions of mind and matter, can be produced to make the impossibility of his escape more complete than it is. —*June*, 1857.

SLAVERY AND CLIMATE.

DOUGLAS will tell you, men of Ohio, that, if you choose to have laws against slavery, it is because your climate is not suited to slave-labor, and therefore you have constitutions and laws against it. Let us attend to that argument for a while, and see if it be sound. You do not raise sugar-cane (except the new-fashioned sugar-cane, and you won't raise that long); but they do raise it in Louisiana. You don't raise it in Ohio because you can't raise it profitably, because the climate don't suit it. They do raise it in Louisiana because there it is profitable. Now, Douglas will tell you that is precisely the slavery question. If that is so, then it leads to dealing with the one precisely as with the other. Is there any thing in the Constitution or laws of Ohio against raising sugar-cane? Surely not! No man desires to raise sugar-cane in Ohio; but, if any man did desire to do so, you would say it was a tyrannical law that forbids his doing so; and whenever you shall agree with Douglas, whenever your minds are brought to adopt his argument, as surely will you have reached the conclusion, that, although slavery is not profitable in Ohio, if any man wants it, it is wrong not to let him have it. — *September*, 1859.

EQUAL RIGHTS.

"IN debating with Senator Douglas, during the memorable contest of last fall, Mr. Lincoln declared in favor of negro suffrage, and attempted to defend that vile conception against the Little Giant." Extract from Ohio "Statesman." "What I did say was in substance as follows: 'I will say, then, that I am not, nor ever have been, in favor of bringing about, in any way, the social and political equality of the white and black races; that I am not, nor ever have been, in favor of making voters or jurors of negroes, nor of qualifying them to hold office, or intermarry with white people; and I will say, in addition to this, that there is a physical difference between the white and black races, which, I believe, will for ever forbid the two races living together on terms of social and political equality.'" — *September*, 1859

STAND BY DUTY.

IF slavery is right, all words, acts, laws, and constitutions against it are themselves wrong, and should be silenced and swept away. If it is right, we cannot justly object to its nationality, its universality; if it is wrong, they cannot justly insist upon its extension, its enlargement. All they ask, we could readily grant, if we thought slavery right. . . . If our sense of duty forbids this, then let us stand by our duty fearlessly and effectively. . . . Let us have faith that right makes might; and, in that faith, let us to the end dare to do our duty as we understand it. — *February*, 1860.

MASON AND DIXON.

IN answer to Douglas's assertion, that there was "a line drawn by the Almighty across this continent, on the one side of which the soil must always be cultivated by slaves." I want to ask your attention to that proposition again: that there is one portion of this continent where the Almighty has designed the soil shall always be cultivated by slaves; that its being cultivated by slaves at that place is right; that it has the direct sympathy and authority of the Almighty. Whenever you can get these Northern audiences to adopt the opinion, that slavery is right on the other side of the Ohio, . . . they will very readily make the other argument, which is perfectly logical, that that which is right on that side of the Ohio cannot be wrong on this; and that, if you have that property on that side of the Ohio, under the seal and stamp of the Almighty, when by any means it escapes over here, it is wrong to have constitutions and laws *to devil* you about it. — *September*, 1859.

WHAT WILL SATISFY THE SOUTH?

THIS, and this only: Cease to call slavery *wrong*, and join them in calling it *right*. And this must be done thoroughly, — done in *acts* as well as in *words*. Silence will not be tolerated. We must place ourselves avowedly with them. Douglas's new sedition law must be enacted and enforced, suppressing all declarations that slavery is *wrong*, whether made in politics, in presses, in pulpits, or in private. We must arrest and return their fugitive slaves with greedy pleasure. We must pull down our Free-State Constitutions. The whole atmosphere must be disinfected from all taint of opposition to slavery, before they will cease to believe that all their troubles proceed from us. — *February*, 1860.

NEGROES AND CROCODILES.

I ANSWER to Douglas's declaration, that, "in all contests between the negro and the white man, he was for the white man; but, in all questions between the negro and the crocodile, he was for the negro." He says, If there was a necessary conflict between the white man and the negro, I should be for the white man as much as Douglas; but I say there is no such necessary conflict. I say that there is room for us all to be free; and that it not only does not wrong the white man that the negro should be free, but it positively wrongs the mass of the white men that the negro should be enslaved; that the mass of white men are really injured by the effects of slave-labor in the vicinity of the fields of their own labor.

The other branch of it is, that, in a struggle between the negro and the crocodile, he is for the negro. Well, I don't know that there *is* any struggle between the negro and the crocodile either. I suppose, that, if a crocodile (or, as we old Ohio-river boatmen used to call them, alligators) should come across a white man, he would kill him, if he could; and so he would a negro. But what, at last, is this proposition? I believe it is a sort of proposition in proportion, which may be stated thus: "As the negro is to the white man, so is the crocodile to the negro; and as the negro may rightfully treat the crocodile as a beast or reptile, so the white man may rightfully treat the negro as a beast or reptile." Now, my brother Kentuckians who believe in this, you ought to thank Judge Douglas for having put that in a much more taking way than any of yourselves have done. — *September*, 1859.

JEFFERSON.

IN speaking of the question of slavery as being something trivial and local, this is an idea, I suppose, which has arisen in Judge Douglas's mind from his peculiar structure. I suppose the institution of slavery looks small to him. He is so put up by nature, that a lash upon his back would hurt him; but a lash upon anybody else's back does not hurt him. That is the build of the man, and consequently he looks upon the matter of slavery in this unimportant light. . . . He ought to remember that there was once in this country a man by the name of Thomas Jefferson, supposed to be a Democrat: . . . that man did not take exactly this view of the insignificance of the element of slavery, which our friend Judge Douglas does. In contemplation of this thing, we all know he was led to exclaim, "I tremble for my country, when I remember that God is just.". . . There was danger to this country — danger of the avenging justice of God — in that little, unimportant popular sovereignty question of Judge Douglas. HE supposed there was a question of GOD'S ETERNAL JUSTICE, wrapped up in the enslaving of any race of men, or any man; and that those who did so, braved the arm of JEHOVAH; that, when a nation thus dared the Almighty, every friend of that nation had cause to dread his wrath. Choose ye, between JEFFERSON and DOUGLAS, as to what is the true view of this element among us. — *September*, 1859.

IS SLAVERY UNIMPORTANT?

DOUGLAS assumes (though without proving it), that slavery is one of those little, unimportant, trivial matters, which are of just about as much consequence as the question would be to me, whether my neighbor should raise horned cattle, or plant tobacco; that there is no moral question about it, but that it is all a matter of dollars and cents; that, when a new Territory is opened for settlement, the first man who goes into it may plant there a thing, which, like the Canada thistle, or some other of those pests of the soil, cannot be dug out by the millions of men who will come thereafter. . . . He ignores the very well-known fact, that we never had a serious menace to our political existence, except it sprang from this thing, which he chooses to regard as only upon a par with onions and potatoes. — *September*, 1859.

SAVE YOUR MONEY.

IF the war continues long, as it must, if the object be not sooner attained, the institution in your States will be extinguished by mere friction and abrasion, — by the mere incidents of the war.

It will be gone, and you will have nothing valuable in lieu of it. Much of its value is gone already. How much better for you, and for your people, to take the step which at once shortens the war, and secures substantial compensation for that which is sure to be wholly lost in any other event! How much better to thus save the money, which else we sink for ever in this war! How much better to do it while we can, lest the war, ere long, render us pecuniarily unable to do it! How much better, for you as seller and the nation as buyer, to sell out and buy out that without which the war could never have been. than to sink both the thing to be sold and the price of it in cutting one another's throats! —*July*, 1862.

EMANCIPATION.

IN a certain sense, the liberation of slaves is the destruction of property, — property acquired by descent or by purchase, the same as any other property. It is no less true for having been often said, that the people of the South are not more responsible for the original introduction of this property than are the people of the North; and when it is remembered how unhesitatingly we all use cotton and sugar, and share the profits of dealing in them, it may not be quite safe to say that the South has been more responsible than the North for its continuance. If, then, for a common object, this property is to be sacrificed, is it not just that it be done at a common charge? — *December*, 1862.

EMANCIPATION WILL NOT REDUCE THE WAGES OF WHITE LABOR.

IS it true that colored people can displace any more white labor by being *free*, than by remaining *slaves?* If they stay in their old places, they jostle no white laborers; if they leave their old places, they leave them open to white laborers. . . . Emancipation, even *without* deportation, would probably *enhance* the wages of white labor; and, very surely, would *not* reduce them. . . . *With* deportation, even to a limited extent, enhanced wages to white labor is mathematically certain. Labor is like any other commodity in the market: increase the demand for it, and you increase the price of it. Reduce the supply of black labor, by colonizing the black laborer out of the country, and by precisely so much you increase the demand for and wages of white labor. — *December*, 1862.

A LETTER FROM HIM HITHERTO UNPUBLISHED.

Gutberth Bullitt, Esq., New Orleans, La.

SIR, — The copy of a letter addressed to yourself, by Mr. Thomas J. Durant, has been shown to me. The writer appears to be an able, a dispassionate, and an entirely sincere man. The first part of the letter is devoted to an effort to show, that the secession ordinance of Louisiana was adopted against the will of a majority of the people. This is probably true; and in that fact may be found some instruction. Why did they allow the ordidinance to go into effect? Why did they not exert themselves? Why stand passive, and allow themselves to be trodden down by a minority? Why did they not hold popular meetings, and have a convention of their own, to express and enforce the true sentiments of the State? If pre-organization was against them then, why not do this now that the United States army is present to protect them? The paralyzer, the dead palsy, of the Government in the whole struggle is, that this class of men will do nothing for the Government, nothing for themselves, except that the Government shall not strike its enemies lest they should be struck by accident.

Mr. Durant complains, that, in various ways, the relation of master and slave is disturbed by the presence of our army; and he considers it particularly vexatious, that this in part is done under cover of an Act of Congress, while Constitutional guarantees are superadded on the plea of military necessity. The truth is, that what is done and omitted about slaves is done and omitted on the same military necessity. It is a military necessity to have men and money; and we cannot get either in sufficient numbers or amounts, if we keep from or drive from our lines slaves coming to them.

Mr. Durant cannot be ignorant of the pressure in this direction, nor of my efforts to hold it within bounds, till he, and such as he, shall have time to help themselves.

I am not posted to speak understandingly on the public regulations of which Mr. Durant complains. If experience shows any of them to be wrong, let them be set right. I think I can perceive, in the freedom of trade which Mr. Durant urges, that he would relieve both friends and enemies from the pressure of the blockade. By this, he would serve the enemy more effectively than the enemy is able to serve himself.

I do not say or believe that to serve the enemy is

the purpose of Mr. Durant, or that he is conscious of any purposes other than national and patriotic ones. Still, if there were a class of men, who, having no choice of sides in the contest, were anxious only to have quiet and comfort for themselves while it rages, and to fall in with the victorious side at the end of it, without loss to themselves, their advice as to the mode of conducting the contest would be precisely such as his.

He speaks of no duty, apparently thinks of none, resting upon Union men. He even thinks it injurious to the Union cause that they should be restrained in trade and passage without taking sides. They are to touch neither a sail nor a pump, — live merely passengers ("dead-heads" at that), to be carried throughout the storm, and safely landed right side up. Nay, more: even a mutineer is to go untouched lest these sacred passengers receive an accidental wound

Of course, the rebellion will never be suppressed in Louisiana, if the professed Union men there will neither help to do it, nor permit the Government to do it without their help.

Now, I think the true remedy is very different from what is suggested by Mr. Durant. It does not lie in rounding the rough angles of the war, but in removing the necessity for the war. The people of Louisiana, who wish protection to person and property, have but to reach forth their hands and take it. Let them in good faith re-inaugurate the national authority, and set up a State government conforming thereto under the Constitution. They know how to do it, and can have the protection of the army while doing it. The army will be withdrawn so soon as such government can dispense with its presence; and the people of the State can then, upon the old terms, govern themselves to their own liking. This is very simple and easy.

If they will not do this, if they prefer to hazard all for the sake of destroying the Government, it is for them to consider whether it is probable I will surrender the Government to save them from losing all. If they decline what I suggest, you scarcely need to ask what I will do.

What would you do in my position?

Would you drop the war where it is? or would you prosecute it in future with elder-stalk squirts charged with rose-water? Would you deal lighter blows rather then heavier ones? Would you give up the contest, leaving every available means unapplied?

I am in no boastful mood. I shall not do more than I can, but shall do all I can to save the Government, which is my sworn duty, as well as my personal inclination. I shall do nothing in malice. What I deal with is too vast for malicious dealing.

Yours very truly,

A. LINCOLN.

WASHINGTON, D.C., July 28, 1862.

PROTECTION TO COLORED SOLDIERS.

AT the commencement of the war, it was doubtful whether black men would be used as soldiers or not. The matter was examined into very carefully; and, after mature deliberation, the whole matter resting as it were with himself, he, in his judgment, decided that they should. He was responsible for the act to the American people, to a Christian nation, to the future historian; and, above all, to his God, to whom he would have one day to render an account of his stewardship. He would now say, that, in his opinion, the black soldier *should* have the same protection as the white soldier; and he *would* have it. . . . When the Government knows the facts from official sources, and they prove to substantiate the reports, retribution will be surely given. — *April*, 1864.

IT IS SIMPLY A WAR-MEASURE.

UNDERSTAND, I raise no objections against it on legal or constitutional grounds; for, as Commander-in-Chief of the army and navy, in time of war I suppose I have a right to take any measures which may best subdue the enemy: nor do I urge objections of a moral nature, in view of possible consequences of insurrection and massacre at the South. I view this matter as a practical war-measure, to be decided on according to the advantages or disadvantages it may offer to the suppression of the rebellion.

GRADUAL EMANCIPATION.

I AM pressed with a difficulty not yet mentioned; one which threatens division among those who, united, are none too strong. An instance of it is known to you. General Hunter is an honest man. He was, and I hope still is, my friend. I valued him none the less for his agreeing with me in the general wish, that all men everywhere could be free. He proclaimed all men free within certain States, and I repudiated the proclamation. He expected more good and less harm from the measure than I could believe would follow. Yet, in repudiating it, I gave dissatisfaction, if not offence, to many whose support the country cannot afford to lose.

The traitor against the general Government forfeits his slave at least as justly as he does any other property; and he forfeits both to the Government against which he offends. — *July*, 1862.

PROCLAMATION OF EMANCIPATION.

How will it operate just now?

IF, now, the pressure of war should call off our forces from New Orleans, to defend some other point, what is to prevent the masters from reducing the blacks to slavery again? for I am told that whenever the rebels take any black prisoners, free or slave, they immediately auction them off! They did so with those they took from a boat, in the Tennessee River, a few days ago. And then I am very ungenerously attacked for it! For instance: when, after the late battles at and near Bull Run, an expedition went out from Washington, under a flag of truce, to bury the dead and bring in the wounded; and the rebels seized the blacks who went along to help, and sent them into slavery, — Horace Greeley said in his paper that the Government would probably do nothing about it.

What *could* I do? — *September*, 1862.

BLESSED ARE THE PEACE-MAKERS.

BUT restore the Missouri Compromise, and what then? We thereby restore the national faith, the national confidence, the national feeling of brotherhood. We thereby reinstate the spirit of concession and compromise, — that spirit which has never failed us in past perils, and which may be safely trusted for all the future. The South ought to join in doing this. The peace of the nation is as dear to them as to us. In memories of the past and hopes of the future, they share as largely as we. It would be, on their part, a great act, — great in its spirit, and great in its effect. It would be worth to the nation a hundred years' purchase of peace and prosperity. And what of sacrifice would they make? They only surrender to us what they gave us for a consideration long, long ago; what they have not now asked for, struggled, or cared for; what has been thrust upon them, not less to their own astonishment than to ours. — *October*, 1854.

UNION OR SLAVERY.

IF there be those who would not save the Union unless they could at the same time save slavery, I do not agree with them. . . .

My paramount object is to save the Union, and not either to save or destroy slavery.

If I could save the Union without freeing any slave, I would do it; and, if I could do it by freeing some and leaving others alone, I would also do that.

What I do about slavery and the colored race, I do because I believe it helps to save the Union; and what I forbear, I forbear because I do not believe it would help to save the Union.

I do not want to issue a document that the whole world will see must necessarily be inoperative, like the Pope's bull against the comet. — *September*, 1862.

FROM WHENCE COME MURDERS?

EACH party WITHIN, having numerous and determined backers WITHOUT, is it not probable that the contest will come to blows and bloodshed? Could there be a more apt invention to bring about collision and violence, on the slavery question, than this Nebraska project is? I do not charge, or believe, that such was intended by Congress; but if they had literally formed a ring, and placed champions within it to fight out the controversy, the fight could be no more likely to come off than it is. And, if this fight should begin, is it likely to take a very peaceful, Union-saving turn? Will not the first drop of blood, so shed, be the real knell of the Union? — *October*, 1854.

APPEAL TO THEIR OWN SENSE OF JUSTICE AND HUMAN SYMPATHY.

THERE are in the United States and Territories, including the District of Columbia, 433,643 free blacks. At five hundred dollars per head, they are worth over two hundred millions of dollars. How comes this vast amount of property to be running about, without owners? We do not see free horses or free cattle running at large. How is this? All these free blacks are the descendants of slaves, or have been slaves themselves; and they would be slaves now, but for SOMETHING which has operated on their white owners, inducing them, at vast pecuniary sacrifices, to liberate them. What is that SOMETHING? Is there any mistaking it? In all these cases, it is your sense of justice and human sympathy, continually telling you that the poor negro has some natural right to himself; that those who deny it, and make mere merchandise of him, deserve kickings, contempt, and death.

And, now, why will you ask us to deny the humanity of the slave, and estimate him as only the equal of the hog? Why ask us to do what you will not do yourselves? Why ask us to do for *nothing* what two hundred millions of dollars could not induce you to do? — *October*, 1854.

LET THE FATHERS ANSWER.

IN support of his application of the doctrine of self-government, Senator Douglas has sought to bring to his aid the opinions and examples of our Revolutionary fathers. I am glad he has done this. I love the sentiments of those old-timed men, and shall be most happy to abide by their opinions. He shows us, that, when it was in contemplation for the colonies to break off from Great Britain, and set up a new government for themselves, several of the States instructed their delegates to go for the measure, PROVIDED EACH STATE SHOULD BE ALLOWED TO REGULATE ITS DOMESTIC CONCERNS IN

ITS OWN WAY. I do not quote; but this in substance. This was right. I see nothing objectionable in it. I also think it probable that it had some reference to the existence of slavery among them. I will not deny that it had. But had it any reference to the carrying of slavery into NEW COUNTRIES? That is the question, and we will let the fathers themselves answer it. — *October*, 1854.

THE STAKE PLAYED FOR.

BUT it is said, there now is no law in Nebraska on the subject of slavery, and that, in such case, taking a slave there operates his freedom. That is good book-law, but is not the rule of actual practice. Wherever slavery is, it has been first introduced without law. The oldest laws we find concerning it are not laws introducing it, but *regulating* it as an already existing thing. A white man takes his slave to Nebraska now. Who will inform the negro that he is free? Who will take him before court to test the question of his freedom? In ignorance of his legal emancipation, he is kept chopping, splitting, and ploughing. Others are brought, and move on in the same track. At last, if ever the time for voting comes on the question of slavery, the institution already, in fact, exists in the country, and cannot well be removed. The fact of its presence, and the difficulty of its removal, will carry the vote in its favor. Keep it out until a vote is taken, and a vote in favor of it cannot be got in any population of forty thousand on earth, who have been drawn together by the ordinary motives of emigration and settlement. To get slaves into the Territory simultaneously with the whites, in the incipient stages of settlement, is the precise stake played for, and won, in this Nebraska measure.—*October*, 1854.

HOW DO WE ACCOUNT FOR THE INCREASE OF THE COLORED POPULATION?

ANOTHER *lullaby* argument is, that taking slaves to new countries does not increase their number,—does not make any one slave who otherwise would be free. There is some truth in this, and I am glad of it; but it is not *wholly* true. The African slave-trade is not yet effectually suppressed; and if we make a reasonable deduction for the white people among us who are foreigners, and the descendants of foreigners, arriving here since 1808, we shall find the increase of the black population outrunning that of the white, to an extent unaccountable, except by supposing that some of them, too, have been coming from Africa. If this be so, the opening of new countries to the institution increases the demand for, and augments the price of slaves, and so does, in fact, make slaves of freemen, by causing them to be brought from Africa and sold into bondage. — *October*, 1854.

CALIFORNIA AND SLAVERY.

IN the fall of 1848, the gold mines were discovered in California. This attracted people to it with unprecedented rapidity; so that on or soon after the meeting of the new Congress in December, 1849, she already had a population of nearly a hundred thousand; had called a convention; formed a State Constitution, excluding slavery; and was knocking for admission into the Union. The Proviso men, of course, were for letting her in; but the nate, always true to the other side, would not consent to her admission. And there California stood, kept *out* of the Union, because she would not let slavery *into* her borders. Under all the circumstances, perhaps this was not wrong. There were other points of dispute connected with the general question of slavery, which equally needed adjustment. The South clamored for a more efficient fugitive-slave law. The North clamored for the abolition of a peculiar species of slave-trade in the District of Columbia; in connection with which, in view from the windows of the Capitol, a sort of negro livery-stable, where droves of negroes were collected, temporarily kept, and finally taken to Southern markets, precisely like droves of horses, had been openly maintained for fifty years.—*October*, 1854.

UTAH AND NEW MEXICO, AND THE SLAVERY QUESTION.

UTAH and New Mexico needed territorial governments; and whether slavery should or should not be prohibited within them was another question. The indefinite western boundary of Texas was to be settled. She was a Slave State; and consequently the farther west the slavery men could push her boundary, the more slave country they secured; and the farther east the slavery opponents could thrust the boundary back, the less slave ground was secured. Thus this was just as clearly a slavery question as any of the others.—*October*, 1854.

RIGHT FIRST, ENFORCEMENT AFTER.

I THINK the authors of that notable instrument (the Declaration of Independence) intended to include *all* men; but they did not intend to declare all men equal *in all respects.* They did not mean to say all were equal in color, size, intellect, moral developments, or social capacity. They defined, with tolerable distinctness, in what respects they did consider all men created equal, — equal with "certain inalienable rights, among which are life, liberty, and the pursuit of happiness." This they said, and this they meant. They did not mean to assert the obvious untruth, that all were then actually enjoying that equality, nor yet that they were about to confer it immediately upon them. In fact, they had no power to confer such a boon. They meant simply to declare the *right*, so that the *enforcement* of it might follow as fast as circumstances should permit.

They meant to set up a standard maxim for free society, which should be familiar to all, and revered by all; constantly looked to, constantly labored for; and, even though never perfectly attained, constantly approximated, and thereby constantly spreading and deepening its influence, and augmenting the happiness and value of life to all people of all colors everywhere.

NO FEAR OF AMALGAMATION IN A FREE STATE.

BUT Judge Douglas is especially horrified at the thought of the mixing blood by the white and black races. Agreed for once — a thousand times agreed. There are white men enough to marry all the white women, and black men enough to marry all the black women; and so let them be married. On this point we fully agree with the Judge; and when he shall show that his policy is better adapted to prevent amalgamation than ours, we shall drop ours, and adopt this. Let us see. In 1850 there were in the United States 405,751 mulattoes. Very few of these are the offspring of whites and *free* blacks; nearly all have sprung from black *slaves* and white masters. A separation of the races is the only perfect preventive of amalgamation; but, as an immediate separation is impossible, the next best thing is to *keep* them apart *where* they are not already together. If white and black people never get together in Kansas, they will never mix blood in Kansas. That is at least one self-evident truth. A few free colored persons may get into the Free States in any event; but their number is too insignificant to amount to much in the way of mixing blood.

SLAVERY THE SOURCE OF AMALGAMATION.

IN 1850, there were in the Free States 56,649 mulattoes; but for the most part they were not born there, — they came from the Slave States, ready made up. In the same year, the Slave States had 348,874 mulattoes, all of home production. The proportion of free mulattoes to free blacks — the only colored classes in the Free States — is much greater in the Slave than in the Free States. It is worthy of note, too, that among the Free States those which make the colored man the nearest equal to the white, have proportionably the fewest mulattoes, the least of amalgamation. In New Hampshire, the State which goes farthest toward equality between the races, there are just one hundred and eighty-four mulattoes; while there are in Virginia, — how many do you think? — 79,775, being 23,126 more than in all the Free States together.

These statistics show that slavery is the greatest source of amalgamation; and, next to it, not the elevation, but the degradation, of free blacks. Yet Judge Douglas dreads the slightest restraints on the spread of slavery, and the slightest human recognition of the negro, as tending horribly to amalgamation.

THE VOICE OF THE MASS OF MANKIND IS AGAINST IT.

SENATOR DOUGLAS remarked, in substance, that he had always considered this Government was made for the white people, and not for the negroes. Why, in point of mere fact, I think so too. But in this remark of the Judge there is a significance, which I think is the key to the great mistake (if there is any such mistake) which he has made in this Nebraska measure. It shows that the Judge has no very vivid impression that the negro is a human; and consequently has no idea that there can be any moral question in legislating about him. In his view, the question of whether a new country shall be slave or free is a matter of as utter indifference, as it is whether his neighbor shall plant his farm with tobacco, or stock it with horned cattle. Now, whether this view is right or wrong, it is very certain that the great mass of mankind take a totally different view. They consider slavery a great moral wrong; and their feeling against it is not evanescent, but eternal. It lies at the very foundation of their sense of justice, and it cannot be trifled with. It is a great and durable element of popular action, and I think no statesman can safely disregard it.

"PRECEDENTS" AND "AUTHORITIES."

JUDICIAL decisions have two uses: First, To absolutely determine the case decided; and, Secondly, To indicate to the public how other similar cases will be decided when they arise. For the latter use, they are called "precedents" and "authorities."

We believe as much as Judge Douglas (perhaps more) in obedience to, and respect for, the judicial department of government. We think its decisions on Constitutional questions, when fully settled, should control, not only the particular cases decided, but the general policy of the country, subject to be disturbed only by amendments of the Constitution as provided in that instrument itself. More than this would be revolution. But we think the Dred-Scott decision is erroneous. We know the court that made it has often overruled its own decisions, and we shall do what we can to have it overrule this. We offer no resistance to it.

SUFFICIENT UNTO THE DAY IS THE EVIL THEREOF.

I MEANT not to resist the admission of Utah and New Mexico, even should they ask to come in as Slave States. I meant nothing about additional territories, because, as I understood, we then had no territory whose character as to slavery was not already settled. As to Nebraska, I regarded its character as being fixed, by the Missouri Compromise, for thirty years; as unalterably fixed as that of my own home in Illinois. As to new acquisitions, I said, "Sufficient unto the day is the evil thereof." When we make new acquisitions, we will, as heretofore, try to manage them somehow. That is my answer; that is what I meant and said; and I appeal to the people to say, each for himself, whether that was not also the universal meaning of the Free States. — *October*, 1854.

"POPULAR SOVEREIGNTY" RETROGRADE.

I ASK attention to the fact, that, in a pre-eminent degree, these popular sovereigns are at this work; blowing out the moral lights around us; teaching that the negro is no longer a man, but a brute; that the Declaration has nothing to do with him; that he ranks with the crocodile and the reptile; that man, with body and soul, is a matter of dollars and cents. I suggest to this portion of the Ohio Republicans, or Democrats, if there be any present, the serious consideration of this fact, that there is now going on among you a steady process of debauching public opinion on this subject.—*September*, 1859.

CLAY AND WEBSTER.

FINALLY, the Judge invokes against me the memory of Clay and of Webster. They were great men, and men of great deeds. But where have I assailed them? For what is it that their life-long enemy shall now make profit by assuming to defend them against me, their life-long friend? I go against the repeal of the Missouri Compromise: did they ever go for it? They went for the Compromises of 1850: did I ever go against them? They were greatly devoted to the Union: to the small measure of my ability, was I ever less so? Clay and Webster were dead before this question arose: by what authority shall our senator say they would espouse his side of it, if alive? Mr. Clay was the leading spirit in making the Missouri Compromise: is it very credible, that, if now alive, he would take the lead in the breaking of it? The truth is, that some support from Whigs is now a necessity with the Judge; and for this it is that the names of Clay and Webster are now invoked. His old friends have deserted him in such numbers as to leave too few to live by. He came to his own, and his own received him not; and, lo! he turns unto the Gentiles.

FAITH.

FAITH.

FAITH IN GOD.—FAITH IN THE PEOPLE.

HOPE.

I AM leaving you on an errand of national importance, attended, as you are aware, with considerable difficulties. Let us believe, as some poet has expressed it, "Behind the cloud the sun is still shining."

JUSTICE OF THE PEOPLE.

WHY should there not be a patient confidence in the ultimate justice of the people? Is there any better or equal hope in the world? In our present differences, is either party without faith of being in the right? If the Almighty Ruler of nations, with his eternal truth and justice, be on your side of the North, or on yours of the South, that truth and justice will surely prevail by the judgment of this great tribunal of the American people.—*March*, 1861.

GOD'S WILL.

DO not misunderstand me. . . . I have not decided against a proclamation of liberty to the slaves, but hold the matter under advisement. And I can assure you that the subject is on my mind, by day and night, more than any other. Whatever shall appear to be God's will, I will do.

FAITH IN OUR FUTURE.

THERE are already among us those, who, if the Union be preserved, will live to see it contain two hundred and fifty millions of population. The struggle of to-day is not altogether for to-day: it is for a vast future also.

FAITH IN GOD.

IF we have patience, if we restrain ourselves, if we allow ourselves not to run off in a passion, I still have confidence that the Almighty, the Maker of the universe, will, through the instrumentality of this great and intelligent people, bring us through this as he has through all the other difficulties of our country. — *February*, 1861.

TOILING UP.

NO men living are more worthy to be trusted than those who toil up from poverty; none less inclined to take or touch aught which they have not honestly earned. — *December*, 1861.

GOD'S SUPPORT OF THE PEOPLE.

IT is a consoling circumstance, that, when we look out, there is nothing that really hurts anybody. . . . And from it we may conclude, that all we want is time, patience, and a reliance on that God who has never forsaken this people. — *Idem.*

THE PEOPLE IN MASS.

WHILE I do not expect, upon this occasion, or until I get to Washington, to attempt any lengthy speech, I will only say, to the salvation of the Union there needs but one single thing, — the hearts of a people like yours. The people when they rise in mass in behalf of the Union and the liberties of their country, truly may it be said, "THE GATES OF HELL CANNOT PREVAIL AGAINST THEM." — *February*, 1861.

GOD AND THE PEOPLE.

I CANNOT but know, what you all know, that, without a name, perhaps without a reason why I should have a name, there has fallen upon me a task such as did not rest even upon the Father of his Country; and, so feeling, I cannot but turn and look for that support without which it will be impossible to perform that great task. I turn, then, and look to the great American people, and to that God who has never forsaken them. — *February*, 1861.

GETTYSBURG.

FOURSCORE and seven years ago, our fathers brought forth upon this continent a new nation, conceived in Liberty, and dedicated to the proposition that all men are created equal. Now we are engaged in a great civil war, testing whether that nation, or any nation so conceived and so dedicated, can long endure. We are met on a great battlefield of that war. We are met to dedicate a portion of it as the final resting-place of those who here gave their lives that that nation might live. It is altogether fitting and proper that we should do this.

But, in a larger sense, we cannot dedicate, we cannot consecrate, we cannot hallow this ground. The brave men, living and dead, who struggled here, have consecrated it far above our power to add or detract. The world will little note, nor long remember, what we say here; but it can never forget what they did here. It is for us, the living, rather to be dedicated here to the unfinished work that they have thus far so nobly carried on. It is rather for us to be here dedicated to the great task remaining before us,—that from these honored dead we take increased devotion to the cause for which they here gave the last full measure of devotion; that we here highly resolve that the dead shall not have died in vain; that the nation shall, under God, have a new birth of freedom; and that the government of the people, by the people, and for the people, shall not perish from the earth.—*November*, 1863.

THE MAJORITY RULES.

THE only dispute on both sides is, "What are their rights?" If the majority should not rule, who should be the judge? Where is such a judge to be found? We should all be bound by the majority of the American people: if not, then the minority must control. Would that be right? Would it be just or generous? Assuredly not. I reiterate that the majority should rule. If I adopt a wrong policy, the opportunity for condemnation will occur in four years' time. Then I can be turned out, and a better man, with better views, put in my place.—*February*, 1861.

THE WOMEN.

I AM not accustomed to the use of language of eulogy; I have never studied the art of paying compliments to women; but I must say, that, if all that has been said by orators and poets since the creation of the world in praise of women were applied to the women of America, it would not do them justice for their conduct during this war. I will close by saying, God bless the women of America!—*March*, 1864.

THE PEOPLE THE ONLY MASTERS.

I CONSIDER that, in view of the Constitution and the laws, the Union is unbroken; and, to the extent of my ability, I shall take care, as the

Constitution itself expressly enjoins upon me, that the laws of the Union be faithfully executed in all the States. Doing this I deem to be only a simple duty on my part; and I shall perform it, so far as practicable, unless my rightful masters, the American people, shall withhold the requisite means, or, in some authoritative manner, direct the contrary. —*March*, 1861.

SUPPORT OF THE PEOPLE.

I DO not say, that, in the recent election, the people did the wisest thing that could have been done; indeed, I do not think they did: but I do say, that, in accepting the great trust committed to me, I must rely upon you, upon the people of the whole country for their support; and, with their sustaining aid, even I, humble as I am, cannot fail to carry the ship of State safely through the storm.—*February*, 1861.

STAND BY THE HELM.

THERE is nothing that could ever bring me to willingly consent to the destruction of this Union, under which, not only the great commercial city of New York, but the whole country, acquired its greatness, except it be the purpose for which the Union itself was formed. I understand the ship to be made for the carrying and the preservation of the cargo; and, so long as the ship can be saved with the cargo, it should never be abandoned, unless it fails the possibility of its preservation, and shall cease to exist, except at the risk of throwing overboard both freight and passengers. So long, then, as it is possible that the prosperity and the liberties of the people be preserved in this Union, it shall be my purpose, at all times, to use all my powers to aid in its perpetuation.

HIS OATH WAS PARAMOUNT.

I AM naturally antislavery. If slavery is not wrong, nothing is wrong. I cannot remember when I did not see, think, and feel, that it was wrong; and yet I have never understood that the Presidency conferred upon me an unrestricted right to act officially upon this judgment and feeling. It was in the oath I took, that I would, to the best of my ability, preserve, protect, and defend the Constitution of the United States. I could not take the office without taking the oath; nor was it my view that I might take an oath to get power, and break the oath in using the power. I understood, too, that, in ordinary civil administration, this oath even forbade me to practically indulge my primary abstract judgment on the moral question of slavery. I had publicly declared this many times, and in many ways; and I aver, that, to this day, I have done no official act in mere deference to my abstract judgment and feeling on slavery. I did understand, however, that my oath, to preserve the Constitution to the best of my ability, imposed upon me the duty of preserving, by every indispensable means, that Government, that nation, of which that Constitution was the organic law.

OUR FATHER WILL DECIDE.

I CAN only say in this case, as in so many others, that I am profoundly grateful for the respect, given in every variety of form which it can be given, from the religious bodies of the country. I saw, upon taking my position here, I was going to have an administration, if an administration at all, of extraordinary difficulty.

It was, without exception, a time of the greatest difficulty this country ever saw. I was early brought to a lively reflection, that nothing would succeed, without direct assistance of the Almighty. I have often wished that I was a more devout man than I am: nevertheless, amid the greatest difficulties of my administration, when I could not see any other resort, I would place my whole reliance in God, knowing all would go well, and that he would decide for the right.

I thank you, gentlemen, in the name of the religious bodies which you represent, and in the name of our common Father, for this expression of respect. I cannot say more.

INTERNAL IMPROVEMENTS.

INTERNAL IMPROVEMENTS.

OBNOXIOUS INEQUALITY.

SO far as they involve "obnoxious inequality," this Capitol is built at the public expense, for the public benefit; but does any one doubt, that it is of some peculiar advantage to the property-holders and business people of Washington? Shall we remove it for this reason? And, if so, where shall we set it down, and be free from the difficulty? To make sure of our object, shall we locate it nowhere? and have Congress hereafter to hold its sessions, as the loafer lodged, "in spots about"?—*June*, 1848.

TONNAGE DUTIES.

"ENOUGH may be done by means of tonnage duties." Now, I suppose, this manner of tonnage duties is well enough in its own sphere.... I know very little, or nothing at all, of the practical matter of levying and collecting tonnage duties; but, I suppose, one of its principles must be to lay a duty, for the improvement of any particular harbor, upon *the tonnage coming into that harbor.* To do otherwise, — to collect money in *one* harbor to be expended on improvements in *another*, — would be an extremely aggravated form of that "inequality" which the President so much deprecates. If I be right in this, how could we make any entirely new improvements by means of tonnage duties? How make a road, a canal, or clear a greatly obstructed river? The idea that we could, involves the same absurdity of the Irish bull about the new boots: "I shall niver get 'em on," says Patrick, "till I wear 'em a day or two, and stretch 'em a little." — *June*, 1848.

MR. POLK'S FIVE PROPOSITIONS.

THE prevailing Democratic errors on the subject, Mr. Lincoln stated as follows: —

That internal improvements ought not to be made by the General Government, —

1. Because they would overwhelm the Treasury.

2. Because, while their *burdens* would be general, their *benefits* would be *local* and *partial*, involving an obnoxious inequality; and, —

3. Because they would be unconstitutional.

4. Because the States may do enough by the levy and collection of tonnage duties; or, if not, —

5. That the Constitution may be amended.

The sum of these positions is, *Do nothing at all, lest you do something wrong.*— *June*, 1848.

AMENDING THE CONSTITUTION.

AS a general rule, I think we would do much better to let it alone. *No slight occasion* should tempt us to touch it. Better not take the first step which may lead to a habit of altering it. Better habituate ourselves to think of it as unalterable. It can scarcely be made better than it is. . . . No, sir: let it stand as it is. New hands have never touched it. The men who made it have done their work, and have passed away. Who shall improve on what *they* did?— *June*, 1848.

ABSTRACTIONS.

I MAKE no special allusion to the present President when I say, there are few stronger cases in the world of "burden to the many and benefit to the few," of "inequality," than the Presidency itself is thought by some to be. An honest laborer digs coal at about seventy cents a day, while the President digs abstractions at about seventy dollars a day. The *coal* is clearly worth more than the *abstractions*, and yet what a monstrous inequality in the prices! Does the President, for this reason, propose to abolish the Presidency? He *does* not, and he *ought* not. — *June*, 1848.

HE THAT OBSERVETH THE WIND SHALL NOT SOW.

ONE man is offended because a road passes over his land, and another is offended because it does *not* pass over his. One is dissatisfied because the bridge, for which he is taxed, crosses the river on a different road from that which leads from his house to town; another cannot bear that the county should get in debt for these same roads and bridges; while not a few struggle hard to have roads located over their lands, and then stoutly refuse to let them be opened, until they are first paid the damages. Even between the different wards and streets of towns and cities, we find this same wrangling and difficulty. Now, these are no other than the very difficulties against which, and out of which, the President constructs his objections of "inequality," "speculation," and "crushing the treasury." There is but a single alternative about them: they are *sufficient*, or they are *not*. If sufficient, they are sufficient *out* of Congress as well as *in* it; and there is the end. We must reject them as insufficient, or lie down and do nothing by any authority. Then, difficulty though there be, let us meet and overcome it.

> "Attempt the end, and never stand to doubt;
> Nothing so hard but search will find it out."

June, 1848.

HIS MITE.

DETERMINE that the thing can and shall be done, and then we shall find the way. The tendency to undue expansion is unquestionably the chief difficulty. How to do *something*, and still not to do *too much*, is the desideratum. Let each contribute his mite in the way of suggestion. The late Silas Wright, in a letter to the Chicago Convention, contributed his, which was worth something; and I now contribute mine, which may be worth nothing. At all events, it will mislead nobody, and therefore will do no harm. — *June*, 1848.

LOCAL IMPROVEMENTS FOR THE GENERAL GOOD.

IF the nation refuse to make improvements of the more general kind, because their benefits may be somewhat local, a State may, for the same reason, refuse to make an improvement of a local kind, because its benefits may be somewhat general. A State may well say to the nation, "If you will do nothing for me, I will do nothing for you." Thus it is seen, that, if this argument of "inequality" is sufficient anywhere, it is sufficient everywhere, and puts an end to improvements altogether. — *June*, 1848.

ILLINOIS AND MICHIGAN CANAL.

NOTHING is so *local* as not to be of some *general* benefit. Take, for instance, the Illinois and Michigan Canal. Considered apart from its effects, it is perfectly local. Every inch of it is within the State of Illinois. That canal was first opened for business last April. In a very few days we were all gratified to learn, among other things, that sugar had been carried from New Orleans, through the canal, to Buffalo in New York. This sugar took this route, doubtless, because it was cheaper than the old route. Supposing the benefit in the reduction of the cost of carriage to be shared between seller and buyer, the result is, that the New-Orleans merchant sold his sugar a little *dearer*, and the people of Buffalo sweetened their coffee a little *cheaper*, than before; a benefit resulting *from* the canal, not to Illinois, where the canal *is*, but to Louisiana and New York, where it is *not*. In other transactions Illinois will, of course, have her share, and perhaps the larger share too, in the benefits of the canal; but the instance of the sugar clearly shows, that the *benefits* of an improvement are by no means confined to the particular locality of the improvement itself. — *June*, 1848.

FEW THINGS WHOLLY EVIL.

THE true rule, in determining to embrace or reject any thing, is not whether it have *any* evil in it, but whether it have more of evil than of good. There are few things *wholly* evil or *wholly* good. Almost every thing, especially of governmental policy, is an inseparable compound of the two; so that our best judgment of the preponderance between them is continually demanded. On this principle, the President, his friends, and the world generally, act on most subjects. Why not apply it, then, upon this question? Why, as to improvements, magnify the *evil*, and stoutly refuse to see any *good* in them? — *June*, 1848.

THE DIFFERENCE BETWEEN "APPLIED FOR" AND "GRANTED."

THE President tells us, that, at a certain point of our history, more than two hundred millions of dollars had been *applied for*, to make improvements; and this he does to prove that the Treasury would be overwhelmed by such a system. Why did he not tell us how much was *granted?* Would not that have been better evidence? Let us turn to it, and see what it proves. In the message, the President tells us that "during the four succeeding years, embraced by the administration of President Adams, the power, not only to appropriate money, but to apply it, under the direction and authority of the General Government, as well to the construction of roads as to the improvement of harbors and rivers, was fully asserted and exercised."

This, then, was the period of greatest enormity. These, if any, must have been the days of the two hundred millions. And how much do you suppose was really expended for improvements during that four years? Two hundred millions? One hundred? Fifty? Ten? Five? No, sir: less than two millions. As shown by authentic documents, the expenditures on improvements, during 1825, 1826, 1827, and 1828, amounted to $1,879,627.01. These four years were the period of Mr. Adams's administration, nearly and substantially. This fact shows, that, when the power to make improvements "was fully asserted and exercised," the Congress *did* keep within reasonable limits; and what *has* been done, it seems to me, *can* be done again. — *June*, 1848.

ALL IMPROVEMENTS LIABLE TO INEQUALITY TO SOME ONE.

NEITHER the President, nor any one, can possibly specify an improvement which shall not be clearly liable to one or another of the objections he has urged on the score of expediency. I have shown, and might show again, that no work — no object — can be so general as to dispense its benefits with precise equality; and this inequality is chief among the "portentous consequences" for which he declares that improvements should be arrested.

No, sir: when the President intimates that something in the way of improvements may properly be done by the General Government, he is shrinking from the conclusions to which his own arguments would force him. He feels that the improvements of this broad and goodly land are a mighty interest; and he is unwilling to confess to the people, or perhaps to himself, that he has built an argument, which, when pressed to its conclusion, entirely annihilates this interest.

MR. POLK AND CHANCELLOR KENT.

IT is no disparagement to Mr. Polk, nor, indeed, to any one who devotes much time to politics, to be placed far behind Chancellor Kent as a lawyer. His attitude was most favorable to correct conclusions. He wrote coolly, and in retirement. He was struggling to rear a durable monument of fame; and he well knew that *truth* and thoroughly sound reasoning were the only sure foundations. Can the party opinion of a party President, on a law-question, as this purely is, be at all compared or set in opposition to that of such a man, in such an attitude, as Chancellor Kent?

WORK TOGETHER.

LET the nation take hold of the larger works, and the States the smaller ones; and thus, working in a meeting direction, discreetly, but steadily and firmly, what is made unequal in one place may be equalized in another, extravagance avoided, and the whole country put on that career of prosperity which shall correspond with its extent of territory, its natural resources, and the intelligence and enterprise of its people.

CONCLUSION.

CONCLUSION.

IN the preparation of this volume, we have been obliged to resist the temptations constantly before us, to enter upon the biography of President Lincoln. We have held ourselves to our leading object, and refrained as far as possible from narrative.

The record of the President's life, as made by himself for Mr. Charles Lanman's "Dictionary of Congress," is in the following words:—

Born, Feb. 12, 1809, in Hardin County, Kentucky.

Education defective.

Profession, a lawyer. Have been a captain of volunteers in the Black-Hawk war.

Postmaster at a very small office. Four times a member of the Illinois Legislature. And was a member of the lower house of Congress.

Yours, &c.,

A. LINCOLN.

It may be convenient to add to these dates the following: —

In 1849, he left Congress. In 1856, he received one hundred and two votes, in the Republican Convention, as a candidate for Vice-President, to run with Mr. Fremont. The Republicans of Illinois named him at the head of their electoral ticket, which did not succeed. In 1858, when a senator was to be elected, he and Mr. Douglas canvassed the State together, in that discussion, which gained a national celebrity, from which we have made so many extracts.

On the 16th May, 1860, in the last year of Mr. James Buchanan's career, the Republican National Convention met at Chicago. On the third ballot, Mr. Lincoln was named its candidate for the Presidency. The following incident is preserved of the announcement of the news to him. Such incidents go far towards illustrating the traits of character which endeared him so truly where he was best known.

The superintendent of the Telegraph Company wrote on a scrap of paper, — "Mr. Lincoln: You are nominated on the third ballot;" and a boy ran with the message to Mr. Lincoln. He looked at it in silence, amid the shouts of those around him;

then, rising and putting it in his pocket, he said quietly, "There's a little woman down at our house would like to hear this. I'll go down, and tell her."

On the 6th of November, 1860, he was elected President. The popular vote gave —

LINCOLN	1,866,452
DOUGLAS	1,375,157
BELL	590,631
BRECKINRIDGE	847,953

Mr. Lincoln, and Mr. Hamlin, the Vice-President, received 180 electoral votes. Mr. Bell received 39; Mr. Douglas received 12; Mr. Breckinridge received 72.

On his journey to Washington, in February, 1861, he was received everywhere with enthusiasm. The rebellion had already broken out, and the country had no hope but in him. It is in this journey that the following anecdotes find place: —

At Northeast Station, he took occasion to say, that, during the campaign, he had received a letter from a young girl of the place, in which he was kindly admonished to do certain things; and, among others, to let his whiskers grow; and, as he had acted upon that piece of advice, he would now be glad to welcome his fair correspondent, if she was among the crowd. In response to the call, a lassie made her way through the crowd, was helped on to the platform, and was kissed by the President.

At Utica he said, "I appear before you that I may see you, and that you may see me; and I am willing to admit, that, so far as the ladies are concerned, I have the best of the bargain; though I wish it to be understood, that I do not make the same acknowledgment concerning the men."

At Hudson he said, "I see you have provided a platform; but I shall have to decline standing on it. I had to decline standing on some very handsome platforms prepared for me yesterday. But I say to you, as I said to them, you must not on this account draw the inference, that I have any intention to desert any platform I have a legitimate right to stand on.

At Philadelphia, information was received which made it certain that even then a plot was laid against his life. This caution probably had reached him, when, at a flag-raising on Independence Hall, Philadelphia, he used these remarkable words: —

"I have often inquired of myself, what great principle or idea it was that kept this confederacy so long together. It was something in the Declaration of Independence, giving liberty, not only to the people of this country, but hope to the world for all future time. It was that which gave promise, that, in due time, the weights should be lifted from the shoulders of all men, and that all should have an equal chance. . . . Now, my friends, can this country be saved upon this basis? If it can, I will consider myself one of the happiest men in the world, if I can help to save it. But, if this country cannot be saved without giving up that principle, I was about to say, I would rather be assassinated upon the spot than to surrender it."

Since his inauguration, his life belongs to the history of the world. In the preceding chapters of this book, we have copied, as largely as our limits allow, from the speeches, letters, messages, and other public documents, which belong to it.

Some more personal traits appear in the following passages: —

TAKES HIS OWN TIME AND HIS OWN METHODS.

I SHALL do less, whenever I shall believe what I am doing hurts the cause; and I shall do more, whenever I believe doing more will help the cause.

I shall try to correct errors, when shown to be errors; and I shall adopt new views so fast as they shall appear to be true views.

I have here stated my purpose, according to my views of official duty; and I intend no modification of my oft-expressed personal wish, that all men everywhere could be free. — *August*, 1862.

PARAMOUNT OBJECT.

AS to the policy I "seem to be pursuing," as you say, I have not meant to leave any one in doubt. I would save the Union. I would save it in the shortest way under the Constitution.

The sooner the national authority can be restored, the nearer the Union will be,—the Union as it was.

If there be those who would not save the Union, unless they could, at the same time, save slavery, I do not agree with them.

If there be those who would not save the Union, unless they could, at the same time, destroy slavery, I do not agree with them.

My paramount object is to save the Union, and not either to save or destroy slavery. — *August*, 1862.

FROM THE PRESIDENT TO HORACE GREELEY.

(Extract.)

IF there be perceptible in it (your letter) an impatient and dictatorial tone, I waive it in deference to an old friend, whose heart I have always supposed to be right.

He is the first President of the United States who has completely abandoned the methods and traditions of diplomacy in addressing himself to the people. He seems to have preferred to explain his policy himself to those whom he recognized as the sovereign power of the nation, in exactly the familiar, even conversational way, in which it would eventually be discussed at men's firesides. From this method of his, and from his profound common sense, it resulted, that almost every address of his, or published letter, really enlightened the public, and gave new courage to the nation. It was often said, that he was the only President who did not injure himself by writing letters. The remark might go much farther. He did not speak often, or write often. He always spoke with freedom, yet never revealed any thing which he meant to keep secret, or which needed to be kept secret. And when he did speak, he almost invariably reconciled, encouraged, or animated the people, who, through the whole country, listened.

From his messages, we have made large extracts. The close of the Message of December 1, 1862, illustrates the same responsibility which is evident in all of them.

WE BELONG TO HISTORY.

FELLOW-CITIZENS, — We cannot escape history. We, of this Congress and this Administration, will be remembered in spite of ourselves. . . . We say, that we are for the Union. The world will not forget that we say this. We know how to save the Union. The world knows we know how to save it. We — even we here — hold the power, and bear the responsibility. In giving freedom to the slave, we assure freedom to the free, — honorable alike in what we give and what we preserve. We shall nobly save, or meanly lose, the last best hope of earth. Other means may succeed: this could not, cannot fail. The way is plain, peaceful, generous, just; a way which, if followed, the world will for ever applaud, and God must for ever bless.

THE INAUGURAL ADDRESS.

This sense of an unbounded responsibility, imposed on the nation and its officers by the living God, is the theme of the Inaugural of the 4th of March, 1865.

FELLOW-COUNTRYMEN, — At this second appearing to take the oath of the Presidential office, there is less occasion for an extended address than there was at the first. Then a statement somewhat in detail of a course to be pursued seemed very fitting and proper. Now, at the expiration of four years, during which public declarations have constantly been called forth on every point and phase of the great contest which still absorbs the attention and engrosses the energies of the nation, little that is new could be presented.

The progress of our arms, upon which all else chiefly depends, is as well known to the public as to myself; and it is, I trust, reasonably satisfactory and encouraging to all. With high hope for the future, no prediction in regard to it is ventured. On the occasion corresponding to this, four years ago, all thoughts were anxiously directed to an impending civil war. All dreaded it, all sought to avoid it. While the inaugural address was being delivered from this place, devoted altogether to saving the Union without war, insurgent agents were in the city, seeking to destroy it without war,—seeking to dissolve the Union and divide the effects by negotiation.

Both parties deprecated war; but one of them would make war rather than let the nation survive, and the other would accept war rather than let it perish: and the war came.

One-eighth of the whole population were colored slaves, not distributed generally over the Union, but located in the southern part of it. These slaves constituted a peculiar and powerful interest. All knew that this interest was somehow the cause of the war. To strengthen, perpetuate, and extend this interest was the object for which the insurgents would rend the Union by war, while Government claimed no right to do more than to restrict the territorial enlargement of it. Neither party expected the magnitude or the duration which it has already attained. Neither anticipated that the cause of the conflict might cease, even before the conflict itself should cease. Each looked for an easier triumph, and a result less fundamental and astounding. Both read the same Bible and pray to the same

God, and each invokes his aid against the other. It may seem strange that any man should dare to ask a just God's assistance in wringing his bread from the sweat of other men's faces. But let us judge not, that we be not judged. The prayer of both should not be answered. That of neither has been answered fully. The Almighty has his own purposes. "Woe unto the world because of offences, for it must needs be that offences come; but woe to that man by whom the offence cometh." If we shall suppose that American slavery is one of these offences, which, in the providence of God, must needs come, but which, having continued through his appointed time, he now wills to remove, and that he gives to both North and South this terrible war as the woe due to those by whom the offence came, shall we discern therein any departure from those divine attributes which the believers in a living God always ascribe to him?

Fondly do we hope, fervently do we pray, that this mighty scourge of war may speedily pass away. Yet if God wills that it continue until all the wealth piled by the bondman's two hundred and fifty years of unrequited toil shall be sunk, and until every drop of blood drawn with the lash shall be paid by another drawn with the sword, as was said three thousand years ago; so still it must be said, that the judgments of the Lord are true and righteous altogether.

With malice towards none, with charity for all, with firmness in the right, as God gives us to see the right, let us strive on to finish the work we are in; to bind up the nation's wound; to care for him who shall have borne the battle, and for his widow and his orphans; to do all which may achieve and cherish a just and a lasting peace among ourselves, and with all nations.

The victories of March and April gave some relief to the tremendous strain of responsibility which had weighed on the President so long. In March he visited the camp before Petersburg and Richmond; and, with his easy and constant desire to maintain personal relations with the people, he sent himself the daily bulletins of victory, from one of which we have quoted the sad prophecy which is the motto of this book.

He had returned to Washington before Lee's surrender. On the night when that news was received, he was called out by an eager throng, who serenaded him, to address them. He made his last long speech. His face, so often sad and careworn, "beamed with a patriotic joy." These are the words of a sensative bystander. The President said,—

"We meet this evening, not in sorrow, but in gladness of heart. The evacuation of Petersburg and Richmond, and surrender of the principal insurgent army, give hopes of a righteous and speedy peace, whose joyous expression cannot be restrained. In the midst of this, however, 'He from whom all blessings flow' must not be forgotten. A call for a National Thanksgiving is being prepared, and will be duly promulgated. Nor must those whose harder part gives us the cause of rejoicing be overlooked; their honors must not be parcelled out with others. I myself was near the front, and had the high pleasure of transmitting much of the good news to you; but no part of the honor for the plan or execution is mine. To General Grant, his skilful officers and brave men, it all belongs. The gallant navy stood ready, but was not in reach to take an active part.

"Nor is it a small additional embarrassment that we, the loyal people, differ among ourselves as to the mode, manner, and measure of reconstruction.

"By these recent successes the re-inauguration of the national authority, the reconstruction of which has had a large share of thought from the first, is pressed much more closely upon our attention. It is fraught with great difficulty. Unlike a case of war between independent nations, there is no authorized organ for us to treat with; no one man has authority to give up the rebellion for any other man. We simply must begin with and mould from disorganized and discordant elements.

"As a general rule, I abstain from reading the reports of attacks upon myself, wishing not to be provoked by that to which I cannot properly return an answer. In spite of this precaution, however, it comes to my knowledge that I am much censured for some supposed agency in setting up and seeking to sustain the new State government of Louisiana. In this I have done just so much and no more than the public knows. In the annual message of December, 1863, and accompanying proclamation, I presented a plan of reconstruction, as the phrase goes, which I promised, if adopted by any State, would be acceptable to and sustained by the Executive Government of the nation. I distinctly stated that this was not the only plan which might possibly be accepted, and I also distinctly protested that the Executive claimed no right to say when or whether members should be entitled to seats in

Congress from such States. This plan was in advance submitted to the then Cabinet, and approved by every member of it. One of them suggested that I should then and in that connection apply the emancipation proclamation to the excepted parts of Virginia and Louisiana; that I should drop the suggestion about apprenticeship for freed people, and that I should omit the protest against my own power in regard to the admission of members of Congress; but even he approved every part and parcel of the plan which has since been employed or touched by the action of Louisiana. The new Constitution of Louisiana, declaring emancipation for the whole State, practically applies the proclamation to the part previously excepted; it does not adopt apprenticeship for freed people, and is silent, as it could not well be otherwise, about the admission of members to Congress. So that, as it applied to Louisiana, every member of the Cabinet fully approved the plan. The message went to Congress, and I received many commendations of the plan, written and verbal; and not a single objection to it from any professed emancipationist came to my knowledge until after the news reached Washington that the people of Louisiana had begun to move in accordance with it. From about July,

1862, I had corresponded with different persons supposed to be interested in the reconstruction of a State government for Louisiana. When the message of 1863, with the plan before mentioned, reached New Orleans, General Banks wrote me that he was confident the people, with his military co-operation, would reconstruct substantially on that plan. I wrote to him and some of them to try it. They tried it, and the result is known. Such has been my only agency in getting up the Louisiana government. As to sustaining it, my promise is out, as before stated; but, as bad promises are better broken than kept, I shall treat this as a bad promise, and break it whenever I shall be convinced that keeping it is adverse to the public interest: but I have not yet been so convinced. I have been shown a letter on this subject, supposed to be an able one, in which the writer expresses regret that my mind has not seemed to be definitely fixed on the question, whether the seceded States, so called, are in the Union or out of it. It would, perhaps, add astonishment to his regret, were he to learn, that, since I have found professed Union men endeavoring to answer that question, I have purposely forborne any public expression upon it. As it appears to me, that question has not been, nor is yet, a practically material one; and thus any discussion of it, while it thus remains practically immaterial, could have no effect other than the mischievous one of dividing our friends; yet, whatever it may become, that question is bad as a basis of controversy, and good for nothing at all.

"We all agree, that the seceded States, so called, are out of their proper practical relation with the Union; and that the sole object of the Government, civil and military, in regard to these States, is to again get them into that proper practical relation. I believe it is not only possible, but in fact easier, to do this, without deciding, or even considering, whether those States have ever been out of the Union, than with it. Finding themselves safely at home, it would be utterly immaterial whether they had been abroad. Let us all join in doing the acts necessary to restore the proper practical relations between these States and the Union; and each for ever after innocently indulge his own opinion, whether, in doing the acts, he brought the States from without into the Union, or only gave them proper assistance, — they never having been out of it.

"The amount of constituency, so to speak, on which the Louisiana government rests, would be more satisfactory to all, if it contained fifty thousand or thirty thousand, or even twenty thousand, instead of twelve thousand, as it does. It is also unsatisfactory to some, that the elective franchise is not given to the colored man. I would myself prefer that it were now conferred on the very intelligent, and on those who serve our cause as soldiers. Still the question is not, whether the Louisiana government, as it stands, is quite all that is desirable. The question is, Will it be wiser to take it as it is, and help to improve it, or to reject it? Can Louisiana be brought into the proper practical relation with the Union sooner by sustaining or discarding her new State government? Some twelve thousand voters, in the heretofore Slave State of Louisiana, have sworn allegiance to the Union, assumed to be the rightful political power of the State, held elections, organized a State government, adopted a Free-State Constitution, giving the benefit of the public schools equally to white and black, and empowering the Legislature to confer the elective franchise upon the colored man. This Legislature has already voted to ratify the Constitutional amendment, recently passed by Congress, abolishing slavery throughout the nation.

"These twelve thousand persons are thus fully

committed to the Union, and to perpetuate freedom in the State, — committed to the very things and nearly all the things the nation wants; and they ask the nation's recognition and its assistance to make good this committal. Now, if we reject and spurn them, we do our utmost to disorganize and disperse them. We, in fact, say to the white man, 'You are worthless, or worse: we will neither help you, nor be helped by you.' To the blacks we say, 'This cup of liberty, which these your old masters hold to your lips, we will dash from you, and leave you to the chances of gathering the spilled and scattered contents in some vague and undefined manner, when, where, or how we cannot tell.' If this course, discouraging and paralyzing both white and black, has any tendency to bring Louisiana into proper practical relations with the Union, I have so far been unable to perceive it.

"If, on the contrary, we recognize and sustain the new government of Louisiana, the converse of all this is true. We encourage the hearts and nerve the arms of twelve thousand to adhere to their work, and argue for it, and proselyte for it, and fight for it; and feed it, and grow it, and ripen it to a complete success. The colored man, too, in seeing all united for him, is inspired with vigilance and energy and daring to the same end. Grant that he desires the elective franchise, will he not obtain it sooner by saving the already advanced steps towards it than by falling backwards over them?

"Concede that the new government of Louisiana is only to what it should be as the egg is to the fowl, we shall sooner have the fowl by hatching the egg than by smashing it.

"Again, if we reject Louisiana, we also reject her vote in favor of the proposed amendment to the national Constitution. To meet this proposition, it has been argued that no more than three-fourths of those States which have not attempted secession, are necessary to validly ratify the amendment. I do not commit myself against this further than to say, that such a ratification would be questionable, and sure to be persistently questioned, while its ratification by three-fourths of all the States would be unquestioned and unquestionable.

"I repeat the question, — Can Louisiana be brought into proper practical relations with the Union sooner by sustaining or by discarding her new State government?

"What has been said of Louisiana will apply to other States; and yet so great peculiarities pertain to each State, and such important and sudden changes occur in the same State, and withal so new and unprecedented is the whole case, that no exclusive and inflexible plan can safely be prescribed as to details and collaterals. Such an exclusive and inflexible plan would surely become a new entanglement. Important principles may and must be inflexible. In the present situation, as the phrase goes, it may be my duty to make some new announcement to the people of the South. I am considering, and shall not fail to act when satisfied that action will be proper."

INTEMPERANCE IN THE ARMY.

IN answer to a delegation of the Sons of Temperance on this subject, the President replied in substance: When he was a young man, long ago, before the Sons of Temperance, as an organization, had an existence, he, in a humble way, made temperance speeches; and he thought he might say, that, to this day, he had never, by his example, belied what he then said. As to the suggestions for the purpose of the advancement of the cause of temperance in the army, he could not respond to them. To prevent intemperance in the army is the aim of a great part of the rules and articles of war.

It is part of the law of the land, and was so, he presumed, long ago, to dismiss officers for drunkenness. He was not sure, that, consistently with the public service, more could be done than has been done. All, therefore, he could promise, was to have a copy of the address submitted to the principal departments, and have it considered whether it contains any suggestions which will improve the cause of temperance and repress drunkenness in the army any better than is already done. He thought the reasonable men of the world have long since agreed, that drunkenness is one of the greatest, if not the very greatest, of all evils among mankind. That is not a matter of dispute. All men agree that intemperance is a great curse, but differ about the cure. The suggestion that it existed to a great extent in the army was true; but, whether that was the cause of defeats, he knew not: but he did know that there was a great deal of it on the other side; therefore they had no right to beat us on that ground.

THE following incident, as related by the Washington correspondent of the "Chicago Tribune," is a touching instance of his genuine goodness of heart, combined with the native simplicity of a country gentleman: —

"I dropped in upon Mr. Lincoln on Monday last, and found him busily engaged in counting greenbacks. 'This, sir,' said he, 'is something out of my usual line; but a President of the United States has a multiplicity of duties not specified in the Constitution, or Acts of Congress: this is one of them. This money belongs to a poor negro, who is a porter in one of the departments (the Treasury), and who is at present very sick with the small-pox. He is now in the hospital, and could not draw his pay, because he could not sign his name. 'I have been at considerable trouble to overcome the difficulty, and get it for him; and have at length succeeded in cutting red tape, as you newspaper-men say. I am now dividing the money, and putting by a portion, labelled in an envelope with my own hands, according to his wish.'"

HONOR TO WHOM HONOR.

LADIES and gentlemen, I appear to say but a word. This extraordinary war, in which we are engaged, falls heavily upon all classes of people, but the most heavily upon the soldier. For, it has been said, "all that a man hath will he give for his life;" and, while all contribute of their substance, the soldier puts his life at stake, and often yields it up in his country's cause. *The highest merit, then, is due to the soldier.*

HIS LAST WRITING.

THE last words written by Mr. Lincoln were addressed to Hon. George Ashmun of Massachusetts. They were written by him after he got into the carriage to go to the theatre, on a card upon his knee, and were as follows: "Allow Mr. Ashmun and friend to come to me at nine, A.M., to-morrow. — A. LINCOLN."

ON the 14th of April, the United-States flag was raised on Fort Sumter, where it had been struck four years before. In the observance of that holiday, the President and General Grant were invited to Ford's theatre, at Washington. General Grant was not able to go. Mr. Lincoln went, though unwilling. "I should be sorry," he said, "to have people disappointed." These are, perhaps, the last words of the President, which may rightly be published to the world.

HIS LAST SPEECH IN PUBLIC.

HIS last speech in public was in response to a serenade, Wednesday night, the night following the passage of the Amendment of the Constitution. President Lincoln said he supposed the passage through Congress of the Constitutional Amendment, for abolishing slavery throughout the United States, was the occasion to which he was indebted for the honor of this call. The occasion was one of congratulation to the country and to the whole world. But there is a task yet before us, to go forward and consummate by the votes of the States that which Congress so nobly began yesterday. [Applause, and cries, "They will do it."] He had the honor to inform those present that Illinois had already, to-day, done the work. Maryland was about half through; but he felt proud that Illinois was a little ahead. He thought this measure was a very fitting one, if not an indispensable one, adjunct to the winding-up of the great difficulty.

He wished the Union of all the States perfected, and so effected as to remove all causes of disturbance in the future; and, to obtain this end, it was necessary that the original disturbing cause should, if possible, be rooted out.

He thought all would bear him witness, that he had never shrunk from doing all that he could to eradicate slavery, by issuing an emancipation proclamation; but that proclamation falls far short of what the amendment will be when fully consummated.

A question might be raised, whether the proclamation was legally valid. It might be added, that it only aided those who came into our lines; and that it was inoperative as to those who did not give themselves up, or that it would have no effect upon children of slaves born hereafter. In fact, it would be urged that it did not meet the evil; but this amendment is a king's cure for all evils. It winds the whole thing up. He would repeat, that it was the fitting, if not indispensable, adjunct to the consummation of the great game we are playing. He could not but congratulate all present, the country, the whole world, and himself, upon this great moral victory.

HIS LAST INTERVIEW WITH HIS FRIENDS.

IN the afternoon of the fatal Friday, the President had a long and pleasant interview with General

Oglesby, Senator Yates, and other leading citizens of his State. In the evening, Mr. Colfax called again at his request; and Mr. Ashmun of Massachusetts, who presided over the Chicago Convention of 1860, was present. To them he spoke of his visit to Richmond; and when they stated that there was much uneasiness at the North while he was at the rebel capital, for fear that some traitor might shoot him, he replied, jocularly, that he would have been alarmed himself if any other person had been President, and gone there; but that he did not feel that he was in any danger whatever.

Conversing on a matter of business with Mr. Ashmun, he made a remark that he saw Mr. Ashmun was surprised at; and immediately, with his well-known kindness of heart, said, "You did not understand me, Ashmun; I did not mean what you inferred, and I will take it all back and apologize for it." He afterwards gave Mr. Ashmun a card to admit himself and friend early next morning, to converse further about it.

Turning to Mr. Colfax, he said, "You are going with me and Mrs. Lincoln to the theatre, I hope." But Mr. Colfax had other engagements, expecting to leave the city the next morning. He then said to Mr. Colfax, "Mr. Sumner has the gavel of the

Confederate Congress, which he got at Richmond to hand to the Secretary of War; but I insisted then that he must give it to you: tell him for me to hand it over." Mr. Ashmun alluded to the gavel, which he still had, and which he had used at the Chicago Convention; and the President, and Mrs. Lincoln, who was also in the parlor, rose to go to the theatre. It was half an hour after the time they had intended to start, and they spoke about waiting half an hour longer; for the President started with much reluctance, as General Grant had gone North, and he did not wish the people to be disappointed, as they had both been advertised to be there. At the door he stopped and said, "Colfax, do not forget to tell the people in the mining regions, as you pass through them, what I told you this morning about the development when peace comes; and I will telegraph you at San Francisco." He shook hands with both gentlemen, with a pleasant "good-by," and left the Executive Mansion, never to return to it alive.

INDEX.

INDEX.